Fargo's Legacy

Tyler Hatch

A Black Horse Western

ROBERT HALE · LONDON

© Tyler Hatch 2012
First published in Great Britain 2012

ISBN 978-0-7090-9834-8

Robert Hale Limited
Clerkenwell House
Clerkenwell Green
London EC1R 0HT

www.halebooks.com

Typeset by
Derek Doyle & Associates, Shaw Heath
Printed and bound in Great Britain by
CPI Antony Rowe, Chippenham and Eastbourne

CHAPTER 1

SUNDOWNERS

They came with the sundown. Not *out* of the sundown but *with* it, riding out of the darkening east, watching the cabin on the high ridge become silhouetted against the sky-fire in the west.

And the two people in the cabin might not even have known that six riders were closing in except for the green-broke roan stallion in the corral. It sensed a mare or two among the newcomers' mounts and pawed the air while it shrilled loudly; reminding them it had, until recently, led the mustang herd claiming, and still running, the high ridges.

The gangling boy hurried to a window, merely curious at first, then, when he saw the intruders spreading out in the ranch yard, he whipped his head around, face white.

'Pa! Riders! Five or six – dismountin' . . . with guns!'

Morgan Fargo strode across the uneven floor of the

room, crouched beside his son. Young Craig felt the stiffness in his father's hard body pressing against him and heard a half-smothered curse, followed by the words:, 'So they've finally come.'

'You know 'em, Pa?'

'Maybe not all of 'em, but there'll be one or two.'

Morgan spoke while he lunged for the fireplace and yanked the Henry rifle down from the antler wall pegs, levering swiftly. 'The cellar, boy! And quick!'

Craig's jaw sagged. 'But – but I'm a fair shot, Pa! I can help.'

'Not against these sons of bitches! Do what I say, boy! And now!' He grabbed his son's bony shoulder and sent him staggering, the single large room now filling with the changing crimson glow of the sun's high-angling rays.

Whatever Craig was about to say next was drowned out by the sudden crack of several rifles out there in the glow of the mountain sunset. Bullets thudded into the logs, at least one splintering part of the window shutter beside the front door.

'Evenin', Morg! Just stopped by to say "howdy!" '

It was a smug, sneering voice that called out of the shadows by the small barn. *Tyson!*

'Been a long time, but I still recognize the voice – Tyson.'

'Bet your britches! We're comin' in! Know you won't be hospitable enough to *in*-vite us, so we're gonna shoot our way past your door – OK?'

'OK if you want a bellyful of lead!'

Craig, standing on the first steps of the cellar ladder,

started to lower the trapdoor, heart hammering as he watched his father blast off a four-shot volley in as many seconds. Just before the trapdoor closed, he heard the startled, agonized shout of a man out there, the hollow clatter as a whining bullet in ricochet punched a hole in one of the big metal tubs hanging beside the barn door.

He gulped, and started to lift the trap again, but without looking around, Morgan said, 'Get down there, boy! And stay there!' He moved fast, stomping on the now closed trapdoor and pulled over the rough deal table, spilling a chair on its side to hide the evidence of any door at all being there.

'Sorry, son,' he murmured. Craig couldn't hear him, nor catch the rise of emotion in his voice. 'Has to be . . .' he added with bitterness. 'Thought the sonuver was dead long ago.'

There were more bullets chewing at the cabin now, splinters and dust flying into the ruddy room. Fargo lunged back and ran to the second window on that side, shouldered the shutter up enough to draw bead with his rifle. He shot a man running near the well, saw him spin drunkenly and sprawl.

Then he fell back with a gritted protest of pain as splinters raked his forehead and face about his eyes. He couldn't see properly but squinted grimly, thrust the rifle out and triggered until the magazine was empty. Fumbling, he reloaded, crouching low, hands shaking.

Goddammit to hell! After all this time, they'd found a reason to come after him! It'd had to happen sooner or later

7

*but with a little luck they wouldn't know about Craig. No! If
they'd found out enough to come here, they would already
know about him . . . wouldn't they?*

Someone kicked at the door, rattling it in the frame.
Morgan rolled on to his side and put two shots
through the planks. A man yelled and there was the
thud and sprawl of a falling body. Fargo rolled swiftly
on to his belly, hearing the rear door smash back
against the wall as someone burst in that way, stumbling.

The man only half straightened before Fargo shot
him through the throat. The man died, thrashing,
clawing at his wound with reddened hands. Another
shape appeared behind him, vaguely silhouetted
against that dark part of the sky. Fargo levered and
reared to his knees but the man had a six-gun in each
hand and both weapons blasted, the muzzle flashes
flickering briefly in the gloom of the cabin.

Morgan spun away and fell on his side, his rifle
firing into a wall,

'I got him!' the man with the twin six-guns yelled,
turning his head so whoever was still alive outside
could hear. 'Still got a couple breaths in him. . . .'

Fargo's rifle triggering from floor level smashed the
rest of the words back into his teeth, the bullet angling
upwards, catching the man under the jaw. What was
left of his face made Fargo wince, though it may have
been pain from his own wounds: at least two in his
body; one high, one low.

Somehow he got up on to his knees, rammed the
rifle butt into his hip and levered and triggered as a

8

man stepped into the doorway.

The man yelled, staggered back, was thrust aside by one of his companions – probably the only one still standing by now. This man stepped forward, fanning a six-gun, the weapon bucking and twisting in his grip.

Fargo crashed against the wall, smoking rifle falling. He hung there, on his knees, kept from falling all the way by one hand on the floor. He looked towards the gunman, mouth working but no words coming – only a flow of blood as he crashed forward on to his face.

The man who came in was medium height, medium build, and had a drooping jet-black moustache that lifted at one side now as his lips curled.

'Been a long time since Hellfire Bend, Morg.'

Fargo lay mostly on one side, hands pressed into his bloody chest. His neck strained as he lifted his head slightly so he could see the man better.

'I – 'member – Tyson . . . also – 'member you – you owe me! Said if ever – I needed – anythin'. . . .'

The words were grating, coming explosively, but quite clear. Tyson arched dark eyebrows, looked puzzled briefly, then gave a crooked grin that made his moustache wriggle, more lopsided this time.

'Aw, yeah! When I got caught up in the raft. . . ? Long, long time ago. You callin' it in?'

Morgan nodded weakly, eyes beginning to glaze. 'Have – to!' Tyson's grin widened, and he laughed briefly.

'Bet you're thinkin' about your kid! Ah-ha! Thought so! That rallied you some, huh? Well, sorry, Morg, old *amigo*! Gotta break my word. I find him, and that shouldn't be too hard, I'll put a bullet in him. Ah, don't look like that! You *know* I have to! We dunno what you've told him, do we? Can't risk leavin' him walkin' around.'

Fargo tried to swear but only coughed blood. Tyson shook his head, kind of sadly, raised his pistol. 'Gotta make sure of you, too!'

He took aim at Morgan's head and, just as his finger tightened on the trigger, he heard a scraping noise and a clatter behind him. Tyson whirled so fast he almost stumbled. 'Huh?' he said as Craig Fargo seemed to rise out of the floor, knocking aside the rough-made chair, a big old Colt Dragoon pistol cocked and clasped in both hands.

The boy's face was pale, but tight and cold-eyed as he fired and the gun's thunder filled the room. The big four and a quarter-pound Dragoon kicked his arms high above his head with the recoil.

When the smoke cleared, Craig saw that the Dragoon had blasted Tyson halfway through the doorway, his broken body sprawled across the stoop, unmoving.

Stifling a sob that threatened to choke him, the heavy weapon still dragging at his right arm, the boy hurried forward and knelt beside his dying father.

'Pa, I – I think we got 'em all.'

Surprisingly, Morgan tried to smile. 'We sure did, son. Come close – somethin' I – I gotta say. . . .'

'Best you don't try to talk now, Pa!'

'*Gotta*! You have to know. . . .'

Fighting tears, Craig leaned close over his father,

using his kerchief to try to stop the flow of blood from the gaping chest wound. Morgan began to gasp out words, his voice trembling, fading, and then, by some mighty effort, strengthening slightly, until it faded once more.

This time it didn't start again.

A great wail of unbearable sorrow wrenched from the boy as he slumped back against the wall, still clasping his father's dead hand.

The moon had risen by the time he had dug the grave on the highest point of the ridge, next to a weathered wooden cross bearing his mother's name, and a date five years earlier. Staggering with fatigue, he wrapped his father's body in burlap, dragged him up the slope and lowered him into the fresh grave. Then he reached for a shovel to start filling it in. *That was the worst part, so . . . final.*

And while he did all these things, he had one nagging thought swirling around in his head: *he had just killed a man! Fifteen years old and he had shot a man dead!*

There had been no choice, because Tyson was in the act of murdering his father, but the deed had only given Morgan a few minutes more of life.

Then something gripped his chest hard as he allowed the thought to intrude now, let it burst through the barrier he had erected while digging the grave and doing the other things necessary. . . .

He shivered, relived the incident, feeling tense and sick. Then he looked at the fresh-turned sod of his father's grave and the first real conscious acceptance of the deed began to form: the tightness in his chest eased, as did the nausea gripping his belly. He hadn't really *saved* his father – albeit briefly; but it suddenly came to him that *he had saved himself!* For it was pretty obvious the man named Tyson was going to kill him after shooting his father.

He was still breathing quite hard but knew that while it might take a while, he was going to be able to live with this thing. There would be no pride in it; it was just something that had *had* to be done and he had done it. There was no other way to look at it – or if there was, he had a notion it would drive him crazy if he allowed it to sit right at the fore of his conscience.

He was not a murderer: that was the thought he had to hold. He sat a while, then went down to the corrals and released the remuda. He stepped aside swiftly as the green-broke stallion charged past, whistling shrilly.

'Go on, you randy jughead! You've earned your freedom!'

Two of the mares followed the roan into the dark between the ridges, but the other mounts milled around the barn, where the horses belonging to Tyson and his men were still tethered. Craig Fargo unsaddled them, let them do what they would: join the grazing remuda or trail after the stallion.

Then he dragged the dead men inside the cabin, collected what he wanted, including the Henry rifle and Dragoon pistol, and splashed coal oil over everything: the walls and the rough furniture he and his father had made together. *A lot of his life was wrapped up in this lonely cabin. . . .*

12

Two vestas tossed into a pool of oil and flames flared hungrily, roaring through the big room as Craig hastily retreated, the heat already searing as the blazing cabin spread its light over the ridge that had been his home for so lone.

By the time he had saddled his usual mount, a medium-sized paint, and lashed his gear on to a docile grey for a packhorse, there was a pale blue line showing in the east.

It heralded the first day of a new life for Craig Fargo. How long that life lasted could only be guessed at as he recalled his father's dying words.

'*Find – those – men, boy, if you want to live!*'

CHAPTER 2

WANDERER

Dark smoke hung against the grey humid sky like a shredded streamer, trailing back from the shaky smokestack of the nine-car freight as the train creaked and clattered its way across the drab, empty land.

Three box cars along from the caboose, a man leaned in the open doorway, flipping a cigarette butt out on to the slope of bluestone gravel that supported the track. He was dark, skin the colour of a rifle butt, and he had big, calloused hands. His youngish face carried a few scars but still he looked young enough to be amiable.

Now he turned his head as another, slightly older man, appeared beside him. This unshaven man had long shoulder-length hair that was mostly straw-coloured, though darkened by grime in a few places where it hung lankly. He sniffed and hawked, spat, but misjudged the wind's direction and the saliva spattered

14

the left leg of his worn jeans. He swore, looked sharply at the younger man. 'The hell you grinnin' at?'

'First thing I learned – and the hard way – when they shanghai'd me aboard that hellship in 'Frisco, was never to spit or toss garbage into the wind.'

'You was a seaman, huh?' the long-haired man's interest momentarily overcame his crankiness. 'That how come you're so dark? Thought you was some kinda 'breed when you first swung aboard.'

There seemed to be a need for some kind of answer and the younger man shrugged. 'Sun'll fry an egg on a cannon out at sea, air's so clear.'

Longhair grunted. 'The sun din' callous up your hands that way – nor cowhand ropes.'

'The ropes I handled were thicker, tougher, stiff with tar and salt.'

The other grunted again, no longer interested. He gestured to the miles of stunted brush and scraggly trees. 'You wouldn't be thinkin' of leavin' us right now, would you?'

'Mebbe.'

Longhair stiffened. 'You serious?' When the other merely continued to stare at him with those hard blue eyes, he shook his head. 'Hell, man, there's nothin' out there but a hundred square miles of scrub and snakes! No one lives out here – not even Injuns.'

The younger man stared out into the quivering blue haze. 'Might be I know of someone.'

'Well, I've heard a few fellers who kinda like to ride with the hooty-owls now and again spend a little time here, but that's only temporary, dodgin' posses.' He

looked sidelong but the other didn't react in any way.
'You're plumb loco if you're thinkin' of jumpin' off
but,' he paused and added in hard-edged voice, 'if you
do, leave your saddle.'

'No.' The other didn't turn his head but the word
came instantly, emphatic, sounded clearly above the
train's clatter and the whistle from the locomotive as
the bored engineer yanked the chain every so often.

Longhair straightened, lantern jaw jutting. 'Well,
now, mebbe that's somethin' we gotta debate. I mean,
we let you share the car with us, and you ate our grub.'

'Stale cornpone and some jerky that'd choke a
toad.' He shook his head. 'Too expensive. That's a
good saddle; old, genuine Spanish-made – had a lot of
care.'

'Yeah.' Longhair turned his head slightly and
nodded to the dark shapes of two other men who had
got to their feet and now stood swaying gently with the
rocking of the freight car. Behind his back, Longhair
gestured with his hand for them to move in on the
younger man.

Some sense warned him and he turned quickly as
the men came at him, reaching for his arms. He
stepped aside and grabbed the skinny one by the shirt
and started to yank him forward to throw him out of
the car. But Longhair and the redhead closed on him,
fists battering.

The young man went down to one knee, head
ringing from a jarring blow, breath cut short by
another. The skinny man he had almost thrown off the
train stumbled back and, in relief at his narrow escape,

16

swore and kicked out. His boot took the other in the chest and he almost went over the edge, one hand grabbing at the metal door slide. Twisting as he hung there, he saw the blurred gravel and stunted brush whipping past a few feet below.

He heaved mightily, wrenching, and the redhead, who had been aiming a kick at his head, instead connected with the edge of the big sliding door which rocked in its track. He howled and grabbed at his skinned shin. Longhair closed and the skinny man managed to land a crack on the young fellow's ear. He rolled into the car away from the doorway and got unsteadily to his feet, swaying with the car's motion and managing it quite easily: no doubt something he had learned as a seaman – moving *with* the roll of the ship. So he was more firmly planted on his feet than the others when Longhair lurched into him, his unsteadiness taking a good deal of the pepper out of his swinging blow.

The youngster's hat fell off, revealing sunbleached hair of medium length. He crouched low, came in under Longhair's next punch and hooked him in the midriff. Longhair gagged and dropped to his knees, trying not to vomit. Almost contemptuously the younger man backhanded him and stretched him out, then turned his attention to Skinny and the redhead.

It wasn't the first box car fight they had been in and while Red feinted and the young man dodged left, Skinny stepped in and hooked him under one ear. He staggered into a barrage of blows delivered with plenty of gusto by Red.

He crashed back against the quivering wall, almost losing his footing with the lurching of the car. He got his guard up as Skinny stepped in, hammering a volley at his face. He weaved and ducked, wrapped his arms about Skinny's waist and thrust his boots against the wall, ramming forward. The thrust carried them clear across the car and Skinny roared in pain as he was crushed against the wall. Red lurched in and drove two crippling blows into the young man's kidneys. His legs buckled and Skinny lifted a knee into his face. He flew backwards into the waiting Longhair, who snarled as he kicked him in the side of the head. It was a good, solid blow and the victim went limp. He didn't have time to fully recover as the three stood over him now, stumbling a little to keep their balance. They kicked and punched him until they were breathless.

They sat down, the young man's prone body rolling and sliding about with the clumsy motion of the box car.

'See if – he's got anythin' – worthwhile on 'im,' slurred Longhair, dabbing at split, bleeding lips.

Skinny and Red searched the unconscious man swiftly, came up with a few dollars, a horn-handled clasp knife with a scrimshawed ship under full sail on one side, and a tobacco sack and cigarette papers. Red swore and kicked out in frustration. 'Got less than we have!'

'Well, we got his saddle,' Longhair said, indicating the rig in one corner. 'Looks good for a few bucks.'

'Yeah, I'd go along with that,' opined Skinny, delving into the sagging saddle-bags. There were some

18

loose cartridges, small screwdriver and a ball of twine with a sailmaker's needle thrust into it. Skinny swore. 'Lousy pickin's! Not even a decent shirt or a damn gun.'

Red had a cut above one eye that wouldn't stop bleeding. He staggered to his feet. 'Throw the son of a bitch off.'

'Was gonna leave it till we got past this.' Longhair gestured to the grey, uninviting country outside the big door. 'Give him some sorta chance to walk out or jump another train. He didn't seem too bad a kid.'

'Hell with that! Throw him off now!' Red said, stooping to grab the limp arms, and starting to drag the unconscious man towards the door. 'I hope he starves or a rattler gets 'im.'

The others both knew Red's meanness and said nothing as they helped to heave the blood-streaked ex-seaman through the doorway. They watched his limp body raise a cloud of dust as it landed on the gravel slope, then skidded into the edge of the brush where it lay still, one arm hooked over a stunted sotol bush.

Red stooped and picked up the weathered wide-brimmed hat that had fallen off their victim during the fight. He sailed it through the doorway, watched briefly as the wind caught it, tumbling it about before it fell and snagged on a grey-leafed brush, ten yards past where the body of its owner lay.

Red dusted off his hands. 'So he won't get sun-stroke.' He smiled crookedly and spread his arms. 'See? I ain't such a mean bastard after all, am I?'

'Red, the way you care for fellers you beat up an'

19

kick half to death, you oughta been a preacher!'
Longhair offered and all three burst into laughter.

There hadn't been rain like this downpour in this
neck of the woods for maybe two years.

It had caught the three ranch-hands off guard.
Their chore was to trap mustangs and brand them
Slash S, but they couldn't work in rain this heavy.
However, they did have a large tarp in the wagon and
so set it up, new-cut poles a mite shaky but holding,
before the worst of the rain hit. Satterlee drew the
short straw and grudgingly dug a deep channel all
round so that it was tolerably dry underfoot inside. All
three stayed close to the small camp-fire, sipping their
coffee and wolfing down the red beans, dipping the
days-old sourdough into the sauce.

Lockie Bruce wiped a hairy wrist across his lips and
reached for the coffee pot to refill his mug. Idly doing
the simple chore, he happened to glance out of the
door flap which had curled back with a gust of wind
and suddenly dropped the pot and swore as he
lurched to his feet.

'Gawda'mighty!' he breathed.

Satterlee muttered and slapped at the lower leg of
his mud-spattered trousers as hot coffee seeped
through. 'Judas H. Priest, Lock! The hell're you
doin'—'

Bruce was staring at the doorway and Price, the
eldest and the ranch foreman, stood quickly, dragging
his Colt out of leather. About then, Satterlee saw the
dark figure working its way in past the folded-back

canvas flap, water streaming from a sodden hat; no poncho, sodden clothes torn and tattered.

'Friend, it is customary to knock your teeth together before intrudin' on a camp after dark in this country!' growled Price, his mostly toothless mouth working, the Colt now cocked. His wiry body was tensed.

'S-sorry,' gasped the newcomer, swaying with obvious fatigue. His face was gaunt, dark, the eyes sunken, though he squinted even in the dim light cast by the small fire. 'Smelled your coffee before I saw the – tent. I – I could sure use a cup an' mebbe somethin' to – to soak it up . . . I—'

The voice was rasping, breathless, a little steam puffing with each word. The man swayed, moved his feet to steady up.

'Can I – come—' The last word was no more than an unintelligible gurgle and he half turned, hand sliding down the sodden edge of the flap, tearing away a little at the top, as he crashed on to his back, half-in, half-out of the door-way.

Lockie Bruce went across and dragged him all the way in. The hat fell off with a plop it was so sodden, revealing the narrow, mud-spattered face of a man in his early twenties.

'He's had an argument with somethin' – or someone,' opined Satterlee, gesturing to the battered face.

'Best get him warm,' Price said and indicated the small pile of old floursacks they used as towels. Satterlee stripped off the stranger's clothes and they dried him briskly, noticing a tattooed anchor with a fouled rope around one of the flukes on the inside of his left forearm.

'Reckon he's a seafarer?'

'Might be. That's a mighty deep tan – look where it stops at his waist! Christ, he's milk-white below his belt-line.' Price pulled a plug of tobacco from his shirt pocket and bit off a piece, jaws chomping, dark juice running-over his chin because he had a few teeth missing. 'Best put a slug of redeye in some coffee; the way he's shiverin' would shake every damn apple off a tree.'

The man responded more swiftly than they expected and in the way of the cattle country they each donated a garment for him to wear. The trousers were a mite short but his worn half-boots would hide that. The undershirt was too tight to be buttoned, but the flannel shirt, once Bruce's, fit snugly enough.

'I'm obliged, gents. Thought I was gonna drown in that damn rain.'

'Where the hell you come from way out here?' Price asked. 'Nothin' but scrub for miles down the slope. This here's the outer limit of the Slash S ranch, by the way. I been workin' it for years, but this is the first time I seen anyone come in on foot from out there.'

The man sipped his coffee, wiped his lips, and the three cowboys all thought the same thing: *He's thinking of what he'll tell us. . . .*

'Fell off the freight train: nowhere else to go but these hills . . . and they looked a helluva long way off.'

'The freight train?' echoed Satterlee. 'Hell, it's two days since it passed through. You sayin' you walked through that there gut-bustin' scrub for two days?'

The man nodded carefully.

'You'da cooked in the heat of the sun!' Bruce said disbelievingly.

The stranger didn't show any offence. 'Walked mostly at night when it was cooler.'

After a brief silence, Bruce once again voiced his scepticism. 'How'd you find your way? You wouldn't've seen these low hills at night.'

'No, just the stars.'

'The stars?'

'Yeah – long as I can find the North Star it's no problem. I'd already glimpsed the hills and knew they were generally sou'-sou'-east from where I was.' His voice trailed as they stared at him. He smiled slowly, sipped some more coffee. 'Damn good brew this. Gents, I'm a sailor. Been nigh on four years at sea and I know how to use the stars.'

That satisfied them, along with the tattooed anchor and the deepwater tan.

Satterlee offered him the makings and he nodded, deftly rolling a cigarette. They noticed his thick, cal-loused fingers and the big, work-hardened hands. He picked a twig from the fire, blew on the glowing end and lit the cigarette.

'You sure got tough-lookin' hands,' opined Price.

'Rope made 'em that way – rope hardened with salt and tar. Ship's rigging. A lot rougher than lariats.'

'How would you know?' Bruce asked without heat.

'I've spent some time on ranches – before they shanghai'd me in 'Frisco.'

'You was kidnapped?'

' "Shanghai'd" is the word, though the seamen don't like you using it, yeah. I was looking for a feller and wandered along the Embarcadero, a long road around the anchorage, when a – a gal took my attention.' He smiled ruefully. 'Just long enough for someone to come up behind me and crack my skull with a cudgel. I woke up with seven other fellers in the stinkin' hold of a sailing ship.'

His voice trailed off and Price asked gently, 'A hellship?'

'With the devil himself as the captain!'

'You said you was four years at sea! Why the hell din' you jump over the side or somethin'?'

'Mister, if you'd been in water above your knees you wouldn't ask such a damn fool question. Where can you go in the middle of the Pacific? Apart from straight into a shark's belly, or down to Davey Jones.'

'Well, you musta had some chances to get away.'

'Yeah, in a couple foreign places, but it ain't so easy if you don't know the lingo and you got no money.'

They were silent briefly while they thought about it. Then Satterlee said, 'Well, ridin' range'll do me. I don't even like deep bathtubs an' I only been on a raft once. No, lotta water's not for me.' He suddenly thrust out a hand. 'Will Satterlee, an' this is Lockie Bruce. The old feller's Price – too damn old to remember his first name!'

'Mine's Craig,' said the stranger, shaking their hands one by one. 'I'm much obliged to you fellers. Er, you mentioned your ranch brand – Slash S? I was heading that way – why I was ridin' the freight. I was told it passed pretty close to Slash S land and figured I could cut across country. Didn't know it was so damn big and downright . . . Godawful.'

'Musta wanted to get here bad,' allowed Bruce.

'Not here – the ranch. Looking for someone named George Sloane. I hear he owns Slash S. That right?'

Bruce said slowly, 'Well, Slash S is a Sloane ranch, but Dusty runs it now.'

'Dunno about no "Dusty", just this George Sloane.' Craig broke off as their faces seemed to change in the dim light: become wary, even suspicious. 'What'd I say. . . ?'

They left it to Price to answer. He said flatly, 'George is dead – we buried him a month ago.'

Craig had gone very still, his face suddenly gaunt. His voice wasn't much above a whisper as he said, 'Ah, hell! Not him, too!'

The trio tensed, glanced at each other. Price started to speak but Craig said with more than a little trace of bitterness, 'How'd he die? Ridin' "accident"? Drown? Fell, or was he pushed off a cliff? Or mebbe he was drygulched. . . ?'

Suddenly Price's six-gun was in his fist, thumb on the hammer spur, his lined face very grave as he asked, 'Just who the hell are you, mister? *No!* Don't bother to answer! You can explain when we get to the ranch. Lockie, get my lariat and hogtie this son of a bitch – and make the rope *bite!*'

CHAPTER 3

SLASH S

No one had mentioned that Dusty Sloane was a woman – and a downright good-looking woman at that.

She was a couple of years older than Craig, wore cowhide working chaps over faded dungarees. She still had spurs on her dusty riding boots. She filled out the checkered blouse the way a woman should, the top two buttons undone.

Craig was standing between Price and Lockie Bruce, hands in front of him. She saw the ropes binding his hands and swung her gaze to Price. She started to speak but then he said, suddenly pointing past her shoulder, and nodding towards the corral, 'Want me to handle that?' There, a big surly ranny was struggling with a wild-eyed sorrel, lifting a coiled lariat threateningly with one hand while he held the rope hackamore with the other. Even as Dusty Sloane yelled, 'Quit that,

Bascombe!' the ranny hit the sorrel a blow with the heavy coil that rocked it on its feet: it wasn't the first blow the horse had taken. Mouth tight, the big man started to swing the coil for a second blow. 'Damn jughead bit my shoulder!' he gritted.

'I said quit it!' Dusty cried, starting forward, but suddenly, Craig broke free of the light grip Bruce had on his arm. He lunged for the corral and they yelled, going after him. Dusty turned, startled, as Craig rushed past her and fumbled the corral gate open. Bascombe saw him coming fast and jumped back, then raised the rope coil ready to swing. But Craig headbutted him in the face, knocking him against the rails. His bound hands grabbed the man's long hair, twisted him around and slammed his forehead against the top rail of the corral.

Bascombe staggered, dropped the rope and fell to one knee. Craig swung a two-handed blow that stretched him out on his side on the soggy ground, gasping. Then Price, Bruce and Satterlee started dragging him away. Dusty frowned as she looked down at his dazed and bleeding form.

'I guess that says it all, Bascombe!' she snapped. 'My feelings exactly! Grab your time and get out. You show your face around Slash S again and you'll be shot!'

Bascombe struggled to his feet, blinking beneath a cut brow that was already swelling and bleeding. His hand had already dropped to his six-gun when he saw Craig Fargo was unarmed.

'Don't!' snapped Price, Colt lifting, already cocked.

Bascome glared, then spat at Fargo. 'You better

clear the county, mister, you know what's good for you!'

Craig merely stared, his hatred of men who mistreated animals plain on his face. Bascombe squirmed a little under that chilling stare and then strode off, throwing over his shoulder, 'To hell with all of you!'

No one said anything as they watched him stride towards the bunkhouse. Satterlee examined the sorrel and told Dusty Sloane that the injuries were only superficial, but could have been more serious. The heavy, coiled lariat could have blinded the sorrel if it had struck an eye.

'We're well rid of Bascombe,' she said as they watched the man lug his warbag from the bunkhouse and stride to the other corrals where his own horse was. She nodded silently to Craig, then flicked her gaze to Price, looking quizzically at the ropes binding his hands. 'And what have we here, Price? A man who stands up for a dumb animal doesn't need to be bound, surely.'

Her grey-green eyes were calm while she patiently listened to Price's explanation. Then she signed to Satterlee to cut the ropes. Brown hair flew loosely in a brief swirl as she ran a hand through it, still looking at Price.

'Calls himself "Craig". Walked into camp outta the rain. Says he was tossed off the mid-week freight.'

Her eyes shifted to Craig's battered face. He was hatless now, fair hair plastered to his skull. 'You walked through that deluge? You must be half-fish.'

'No, ma'am, just din' see no other way.'

Maybe there was the slightest of nods acknowledging his resolve. 'Why the ropes, Price?'

'Says he wanted to see George. When I told him he was dead, he asked how he died – suggested every which way except natural causes: ridin', fallin' off a cliff, though he said "mebbe thrown". Drygulchin' was his last guess.'

Dusty's eyes narrowed and Craig saw she was tensed now: after all, George had been her father. 'Why did you choose those things for the way my father died?'

The ropes fell away and Craig grimaced as he rubbed briskly when the circulation began to return, tingling and burning. They watched Bascombe ride off, deliberately taking his temper out on his mount by raking viciously with his spurs. Craig tightened his lips as he turned back to the girl. 'Ma'am, it's a long story.'

'None of us is going anywhere right now – including you. Or maybe especially you.'

He sighed and she urged them all up to the porch where they sat while Craig rubbed his tingling wrists. 'Name's Craig Fargo. Lived with my parents in a cabin atop Resurrection Ridge: that's in the Muggyown Rim country, Arizona.'

'We know our geography,' growled Price.

Fargo nodded. 'Bunch of men attacked our cabin, killed Pa – I never did find out why for sure. Ma had been dead five years by then and before Pa died he told me I should look for six men. There was a paper in the cabin that had their names and last known addresses on.'

'Why?' Dusty asked.

29

'He said to tell 'em what'd happened and they should – take care of me. I was only fifteen at that time.'

'Take care. . . ?' How was that meant?'

'How it sounds. Look out for me, help me grow up, I guess, keep me from getting killed, too.'

'How come these raiders didn't kill you?' Price asked, eyes penetrating.

'They tried, but I shot the feller who was tryin' to finish Pa. He was the last one. Pa'd nailed the others.'

They waited, without comment. Finally, Dusty said, 'Your father must've had a lot of faith in you to trust something like that to a 15-year-old.'

His eyes narrowed. 'Didn't have much choice, ma'am. He died a few minutes later.'

Dusty's cheeks burned for a moment and she nodded. 'I'm sorry. Did he have time to tell you why he wanted you to find these men?'

Craig shook his head, 'He just said to tell 'em Tyson led the raid, so beware.'

'Who's Tyson?' Price asked.

'Dunno, but he knew Pa. "Long time ago", was mentioned. Could've been squaring an old score, just dunno.'

'Did you have any success, finding these men. . . ?'

'Some. First two I located turned out to be brothers, buffalo hunters. They didn't ask questions after I told 'em what'd happened. They just took me with 'em out on to the Staked Plains, Texas, for a season. Taught me how to run down buffalo: hunting from horseback, shooting with a Sharps Big Fifty from a stand, how to skin – even had me elbow deep in the innards to get at the liver and other sweetmeats for the Indian helpers.'

'All right!' Dusty snapped, maybe a mite queasy. 'Stick to the facts: we don't need graphic descriptions.'

He smiled thinly. 'Well, we took a load of hides to Fort Griffin. They left me at the camp outside town with the Indians who skinned and salted the hides while they looked for a buyer. They never came back. Both of 'em were killed in a gunfight. Several men claimed it was a set-up – feller named Al Bisby; a known gunslinger, provoked 'em till they went for their guns. One of 'em died outright, the other took a day or so. Long enough to get word to me to ride out and keep riding. Even told me where I might find the next name on Pa's list.' Craig paused and heaved a small sigh. 'Won't go through it all, but just take my word for it when I tell you that before I got to that feller, someone ran him off a cliff. All the sign was there, but they never found who or why. I was getting pretty leery by this time, but moved on to the next name. It took me three months to track him down: found his headboard in Boot Hill at Paxton Springs, New Mexico. He'd drowned in the river three weeks earlier, trying to cross at a safe place used by most everyone. Theory was he fell off his hoss and hit his head on a rock.'

'I think I'm beginning to see why you asked such questions about the manner of my father's death,' Dusty said slowly. 'The remaining two men on your list. . . ?'

'Well, Pa wasn't much of a hand at reading or

31

writing and no one I asked could quite make out the last name: Winston, Winslow, Wilson, Williams – all wild guesses. One feller, tryin' to be smart, even suggested "Winfield". That got a laugh – you likely know Martin Winfield's some kinda politician in Washington? Mighta been funny, but it didn't do me no good. Anyway, I went looking, picked up a trail in Flagstaff that led me all the way to San Francisco.' He paused, as Dusty rose, went to a cupboard and brought out a bottle of whiskey and four glasses. She poured him a drink. Craig sipped gratefully as she gestured for Satterlee and the others to help themselves. She didn't take a drink herself. The whiskey felt good on Craig's dry throat.

'My luck ran out.' He finished the drink and shook his head when Dusty gestured to the bottle, offering another. 'Never got to find my man, because I was shanghai'd; woke up with a fat head on board a damn Boston whaler that'd lost a mast in a storm and limped into 'Frisco under jury-rig for repairs. Half the crew deserted so they sent out a gang to grab anyone who looked fit enough to walk upright. Nigh on four long, brutal years I put in on that goddamn ship before I found a chance to get away.' He paused and they could see he was remembering that escape and the hell he had left behind. But he didn't go into details. 'That was six months ago.'

'An' you took up where you left off?' asked Price, squinting. 'Went after the last of the men on your list?'

Craig nodded. The silence dragged on and the cowboys looked at Dusty. She frowned, her gaze steady.

32

'I take it my father's name was on that list, too?'

'Yeah – just general, you know, like, "G. Sloane, said to be living in Dixon County, Colorado". Enough to set me searching.'

She looked steadily at Craig. 'And you ended up here at Slash S – once again, too late.'

He started to speak, but heard the catch in her voice and merely nodded.

After a short silence, she said quietly, 'I understand now why you asked those questions about how my father died . . . you thought he may've been murdered, too.'

'Well, all I seemed to be finding were dead men.' He raked his gaze around the trio of cowhands and back to the girl. 'Can you help me out? I'm not tryin' to upset you, or muddy-up your father's name, ma'am. I just aimed to check with him to see if he'd known *my* father – and the others.'

Price turned to Dusty. 'Figure we owe him that much, Dusty – we treated him a mite rough. . . ' He almost smiled for a fraction of a second: nearest thing to an apology Craig could expect. Or wanted. 'Wouldn't want you to get the wrong idea about Southern hospitality, kid.'

Craig held up his glass. 'Seems all right to me – so far.' He looked directly at Dusty. 'How *did* your father die? If it ain't too painful to talk about, ma'am. . . .'

She took a deep breath, flicked her eyes at Price. 'It's still hard to talk about, but we found him crushed under a tree he had been felling – an obvious accident.' She flicked hard eyes to Price. 'Though Price

33

has a theory he had been knocked out first, lined up with the tree, and then . . . the tree was dropped on him.'

She stopped abruptly as her voice broke and Craig saw her blouse front rising and falling with her quickened breathing as she remembered her father's death. He didn't know what to say, fiddled with his glass, looking down at the table top.

As the silence dragged, Craig cleared his throat and asked Price, 'How could you tell he'd been knocked out first? I mean a tree falling on him would've cr—'

Dusty, pale now, turned abruptly and left the porch.

Price swore. 'Damn you, kid! You coulda asked me on the quiet!'

Craig nodded. 'Yeah, I guess so. It's just that I've been trailing these men for so long. I mean, even when I was on board that stinkin' whaler, I wondered just *why* Pa expected them to take care of me. I never got a chance to ask any but the two buffalo hunters.'

'What'd they say?'

'Mostly how much they owed Pa and they'd do anything for him. He'd apparently saved their lives durin' the war, but they didn't talk much at the best of times and never did tell me the details. And I never got to even speak to the others! Someone was ahead of me every step of the way, killing 'em.' He turned towards Price again. 'You ain't told me yet why you figure that tree didn't fall accidentally on Mr Sloane.'

'Because George built Slash S up from a piddlin' spread his father left him. He was a real pioneer: he knew what he was about, clearin' land. Someone slugged him and used the axe to finish cuttin' down that tree and dropped it right on him. There were two sets of different chop marks on the stump.'

'You could tell that?'

Price curled a lip. 'Anyone who's got their wits about 'em and worked as long as I have for George Sloane could see the difference. A lot of them fresh cuts had been made by a southpaw, too, and George sure wasn't that! 'Sides, I checked him good. There was a half-moon wound in the back of his head, like the shape left by the edge of a gun butt.'

Satterlee nodded. 'I seen it, too – Price showed me.'

'But not Dusty?'

'Hell, would you? George was squashed under a goddamn twenty-foot tree, for hell's sake! I've seen prettier sights. That gal was knocked clear off her feet by his death,. She'd only been talkin' with him an hour earlier.'

Bruce corrected him in his slow drawl. 'She'd *argued* with him – about some heifers and where best for 'em to graze. Feisty folk, the Sloanes, and Dusty is her father's daughter. I guess it got outta hand a mite – cut her up bad when he was found dead. I figure she regretted some of the things she'd said when they argued and she never got a chance to take 'em back.'

'Hard thing to do – take back what's already been said.'

Price nodded, stood up. 'I guess we can find you a better outfit than them rags you're wearin'. I figure Dusty'll want you to stick around for a couple days, give her a chance to make up for the way we treated you.'

'I've got no real complaint, but I wouldn't mind a chance to rest-up. Feel like I been caught in a stampede.'

'Then what?' Price asked.

'Still got one name on my list. If I can decipher it.'

'You're gonna keep lookin'?' Bruce seemed surprised.

'I promised Pa.' His voice had a hard edge to it that surprised the cowboys. 'I was kinda interrupted in my search – I've thought since that mebbe the years I spent at sea might even've saved my life: I kinda just disappeared. Must've had 'em wonderin' what'd happened to me.'

Price said flatly, 'Well, they must know you're back 'cause they've started huntin' down the men you never reached before you disappeared. Must've figured they didn't need to worry about the other fellers if you were gone. . . . Which could mean you're the key to the whole damn thing.'

Craig Fargo stiffened, frowning, then nodded slowly.

He hadn't consciously realized it earlier, but he saw now that he, too, must be on someone's kill list. . . .

And close to the top!

CHAPTER 4

NEXT OF KIN

Craig slept for twelve hours in a small room at the rear of the main house. When he awoke he was still stiff, sore and bruised.

A shy Mexican maid lightly tapped on his door before opening it. She looked at him with big eyes and asked, dark eyebrows arching, '*Bañera, señor?*'

His Spanish was a mite rusty, not having used it hardly at all while at sea, but he worked out she was asking if he would like a bath.

Just the thought of it seemed to relax some of his knotted, aching muscles. He forced a smile with his split lips.

'*Sí, sí! Bueno, señorita! Muy caliente!*' She smiled and he added, mostly to himself, 'Hotter the better. . . .'

A deep galvanized iron hip-tub was brought in by two Mexican boys who returned a few minutes later with buckets of hot water.

'Keep 'em comin', *muchachos*,' he told them, now stripped and stepping in gingerly, accepting the yellow bar of kerosene soap and a washcloth from one of the boys with a wink and a nod.

He gasped as the heat took his breath away and the kids grinned and left with the empty pails – which he hoped they would refill: he planned to soak for at least an hour.

Then what? he asked himself.

That would be the interesting part.

The same young Mexican maid who had arranged his bath brought an armful of clothing donated by Slash S ranch hands. It wasn't a particularly generous act, just one of those unwritten 'codes' adhered to by men who rode the range in wild country, and knew what it was like to live with a minimum of everything: grub, money, bullets, clothes, bedrolls.

They fit well enough though were a little baggy on his rangy frame. But he was mighty grateful and told Dusty Sloane so when the maid showed him into the big kitchen, where Dusty waited with the Mexican cook.

He still moved stiffly and with a limp as a result of the beating he had taken in the freight car – not to mention the ordeal of being thrown out of the moving train.

The cook set a platter down with a sizzling steak, two fried eggs, two fist-sized potatoes cooked in their skins and a mound of fresh green peas – he had noticed a vegetable garden down near the big barn when he had first arrived.

Dusty let him eat with a gusto that left him feeling mildly embarrassed. After his third cup of coffee, she pushed a packet of cheroots across the table. 'Price said you smoke.'

'Much obliged, er – what do I call you?'

'Everyone calls me Dusty.' She pulled out a chair and sat down at the table as he lit one of the cheroots, looking at him carefully. 'You don't carry any excess weight, do you?'

'Not after working on a Down-easter whaler.'

'But you've been ashore for some time now, haven't you?'

He shrugged. 'Got used to living on a minimum of grub, er, not includin' that elegant meal I've just eaten.'

She smiled faintly. 'What're your plans?'

'Well, ma'am – Dusty – I was hoping you might offer me a job.' She arched her eyebrows in genuine surpise. 'I've worked with cattle and horses, on both ranches and trail herds – and you fired a man just after I arrived.'

'That bad-tempered pig, Bascombe? He should never be within a mile of any ranch. I hadn't planned to replace him, at least not right away, but if you really know ranch work, well, I could give you a try.'

'Thanks, Dusty – and again for the clothes.'

She was watching him closely now. 'You'll need guns, riding the range. I can get you a six-gun and a rifle, but I may take something out of your pay for them.'

He spread his hands. 'OK by me. I better make it clear that I won't be here permanent. Just want to get a few dollars together and be on my way.'

'To find that last name on your list?' He nodded silently. Dusty stood up abruptly, went to a cupboard and brought back a hat, which he had difficulty in recognizing as the one he had been wearing when he was thrown off the freight train. It had been a squashed, sagging wet mess when he had last worn it after regaining consciousness; almost pulped by the heavy rain. Now the brim was flat and tolerably stiff again and the head section was pretty well shaped around newspaper, hard-packed to form a good crown that was close to the original.

He took it slowly and turned it over. He stiffened slightly as he looked up at her sharply. 'What happened to the inner band? It'll fall down over my eyes without that.'

She smiled and nodded slowly. 'The stitching had broken away – it was a very amateurish job.' She paused. 'You should've had it done by someone who could handle a needle and thread and it might not've been so noticeable.'

He smiled slightly. 'Folk who can handle needles and thread ain't exactly in my circles, Dusty. Only one I know who could've done the kind of job it needed was the old sailmaker on the ship.'

'You hid some papers behind the inner band.'

He sighed. 'Yeah, I'd carried those papers of Pa's with the names of the men for a long time, managed to hang on to 'em all those years. Had to fight a big

Swede to a standstill once, on the flensing deck, to get 'em back. He thought I'd pay cash for 'em.' She looked at him sharply, and then warily. He didn't appear to notice. 'When I reached the States again and bought some Western clothes and so on, I figured the papers'd be safe if I sewed 'em into the hat. They were mighty worn and greasy by that time but I figured I should keep 'em.'

'That deluge didn't make them any more legible.' Dusty took a small buckskin wallet out of her shirt pocket and handed him a thick fold of grimy paper. 'Be careful how you handle them – the pages might still be weak after all that water. I had Maria use a flat iron on them between sheets of brown paper, but as you'll see, the writing is almost entirely unreadable now.'

He had already opened the bundle and looked sadly at the mess of smeared blue ink that was all that was left of his father's awkwardly written notes. He sighed.

'Well, I tracked down six outta seven – guess the last one'll have to remain a mystery an' take his chances.'

'I'm sorry, Craig. It's the best we could do, but I doubt if you'll be able to get anything worthwhile out of it now.'

'It's a mess, all right.' He looked up slowly and shrugged. 'Mebbe I'll be doing the last man a favour if I can't decipher his name. If I don't go looking for him, they might let him live.'

'You'll never know then what your father had in mind.'

'No,' he said curtly, uneasy as he suddenly thought she might consider that he was the cause of her father's death: if he hadn't come looking for George Sloane, he might still be alive. 'Pa had kept track of 'em over the years – you can just make out where he'd crossed out some addresses and added new ones. I guess he really wanted to know where he could get in touch if he needed to.'

'Have you any idea why?'

He shook his head. 'Pa didn't have much time to – go into a lot of detail.'

She read the sadness in his face, heard it in his slow speech. Her hand reached out across the table and gently rested on his. 'I'll help in any way I can.' He looked at her quickly and she added, 'I have a stake in this, you know.'

'Yeah, I'm sorry I didn't get here fast enough to I keep your father from getting killed.'

She nodded and her eyes briefly went out of focus, but she pulled herself back to the moment. 'I – I think I have to believe Price now when he says it wasn't an accident, but what's done is done. If you feel up to it, I can give you your first job for Slash S right now.'

He was a little surprised but nodded. 'Sure, I'm broke and eager to start earning.'

'Right. You can drive me into town in the buckboard. I've had word that the stonemason finally has the headstone ready for Dad's grave.' She paused and he heard a long breath hiss through her nostrils. 'I'd like to have it set in place as soon as possible.'

'Be glad to help.'

But he couldn't quite shake a mild feeling of guilt.

The town was called Rio Blanco, and was built on the Roan Plateau in a wide, deepwater bend of the White River.

It sprawled, the streets wide, big gaps between the buildings, as if it was a town waiting to be developed so it could begin to fully function.

As Craig tooled the clattery buckboard down Main, following Dusty Sloane's directions to the stonemason's yard, he noticed the slow pace of the townsfolk; all the benches and the boardwalks themselves were lined with indolent men in range clothes. A drowsy, easy-going place, it seemed to him.

'It begins to come alive just before sundown of a Saturday,' she told him with a wry smile. 'Don't let the sleepy look fool you. This can be a wild place on paydays.'

'I believe it – seen misleadin' towns like this before.'

Then she suddenly indicated a side street they had almost passed and he stood on the brake and yanked the reins hard. The buckboard careered in a tight turn, the wheels spraying dust, one side lifting off the ground a little.

A bunch of lounging cowboys on a saloon veranda hastily covered their drinks as the dust swirled among them and several men shouted at Fargo, not worrying about their choice of words or how they might affect Dusty. She was used to hearing the rough talk of men, but it still didn't sit easy with Fargo – nor did the names they called him.

He hauled rein and, as the vehicle slowed, the wheels skidding and raising even more dust, the girl snapped, 'Keep going!' She forced a smile for the angry men. I'll buy you a round of drinks to make up for those we just spoiled.'

'You don't have to do that,' Fargo said.

'Be quiet! I don't want trouble – or perhaps you haven't recognized Bascombe in that bunch.'

He hadn't noticed the big, surly cowboy towards the rear of the group but he did now as she pointed him out, face bruised and swollen lopsidedly. Bascombe obviously recognized him, too, and let go with a stream of ear-bending expletives as he turned to his companions. Fargo saw the raw cut on the man's swollen forehead from where he had slammed him against the corral rail, as Bascombe lifted a finger and touched it gently.

'Well, I'll be dogged! It's the son of a bitch who took my job!'

'And beat the crap outta ya!' someone said, getting a brief laugh.

'*You* lost your job because of your mean handling of my horses, Bascombe!' Dusty retaliated, trying to get Fargo to keep the team moving.

'Mebbe I should've handled you the same way.'

The men liked that and guffawed. More drinkers were attracted by the raised voices and soon the saloon veranda was crowded.

'*Move*, damn you!' Dusty gritted. 'Do you want a beating at Bascombe's hands, you fool!'

Fargo said nothing, looped the reins over the brake

44

handle and dropped to the ground by the front wheel of the buckboard. Bascombe, forty pounds heavier and a couple of inches taller – and far more experienced in the eye-gouging, bone-crushing style of fighting, or so he believed – was eager to get his hands on Fargo.

'Hope you'll pay his medical bills, Dusty, 'cause he's gonna have a helluva lot of 'em!'

'Just leave it, Basc—'

But Bascombe had lunged at Fargo, moving fast for a big, overweight man who probably had five or six beers under his belly-straining belt, making him a mite more reckless than he ought to be. His big fist whistled towards Fargo's face and the young seafarer lifted his guard. But Bascombe grinned and ducked, changing direction so his punch landed under Fargo's ribs.

The impact lifted his feet off the ground and there was a sigh from the crowd. They knew Bascombe's reputation and figured Fargo would go down and be at the mercy of the mean-tempered wrangler's big, size-eleven boots.

Fargo did go down, half dropping, half twisting, and hurling himself to one side. Bascombe blinked as Fargo shoulder-rolled, bounced up and lunged back towards him with a long stride and a looping punch that was never intended to land – only take Bascombe's attention while Fargo's boot heel slammed down on the big man's instep. His dusty boots afforded little protection and he yelled and danced wildly as his foot bones creaked and gave way. While he was off-balance, Fargo moved around him,

45

jabbing with a left, another left, and yet a third, and as the big bearded head snapped back, the right came whistling in like a cedar log hurtling off the end of a long, downhill chute. Bascombe's head bent back so far someone later said they thought it was hinged. The big wrangler hit the ground hard, blood smearing his mouth, his nose hammered way over to the left side of his face. There was a brief, stunned silence, and then the men were shouting at Bascombe to get up:

'Stand up an' fight like a man!'

'What you doin' down there, Bas? Lookin' for some of your teeth?'

'C'mon, Bas! You can beat this kid!'

'Hell, yeah! You've beat up a lotta kids in your time!'

The taunts must have gotten through Bascombe's ringing head – and the red pain of his busted nose. He thrust erect with a roar, swinging a hand up and hurling gravel into Fargo's face.

Fargo dodged but some stones caught him, tearing his cheeks, forcing him to wrench his head back to save his eyes.

That was when Bascombe moved in for the kill.

Fargo stepped back, brought up against a saddled horse at the hitchrail. Bascombe's fist skidded off his jaw as the animal shied, whickering, jostling Fargo roughly in its panic. As he turned to instinctively grab at the saddle to keep from falling, the horse whinnied and plunged again but the reins held it fast to the rail.

And Fargo found his face up against a coiled lariat hanging on the saddlehorn. He whipped it off in a flash and turned to meet Bascombe's bulling charge.

The heavy coil of rope caught the big man across the side of the head and knocked him sideways. He stumbled, half running for a short distance in an effort to keep his balance. Fargo went after him, swinging the rope back and forth across the man's shoulders and head, turning his face into raw meat.

'You like it, Bascombe?' Fargo gasped, slamming the lariat coils once more, driving the man to his knees. 'That Slash S sorrel's gonna need stitchin' and lose a couple teeth – and so'll you!'

Bascombe was cowering now, covering his head desperately with his arms, blood dripping to the dust. Fargo kept swinging, back and forth, back and forth, the rope ripping the shirt off Bascombe's back, tearing his ears, cutting up his ugly face.

'For God's sake, Craig! That's enough!'

Craig swayed and rounded fast, the wild anger fading swiftly so that he stopped in time from slamming the bloody rope into Dusty Sloane as she clung to one of his arms.

'*Enough*, I said! You'll kill him.'

He looked down at the cowering, bloody, moaning wreck in the dust at his feet, stared a long moment, then nodded and dropped the rope on Bascombe's heaving back. He raked his hard gaze around the mob of silent men, then allowed Dusty to lead him back to the buckboard.

'That was – terribly brutal!' she said curtly, obviously upset.

'You don't last long on a whaler by actin' like you just came outta Sunday school. You toughen up quick or you soon find out what it's like to drown in the middle of the ocean with your ship sailing off and not havin' a notion in hell of even looking for you.'

He helped her up into the seat and swung stiffly up himself, taking the bandanna she handed him and mopping his own bleeding face wounds.

'You've made yourself a terrible enemy, you know.'

He laughed shortly. 'Hell, Bascombe wouldn't've lasted a week on that whaler. They'd've fed him into the boiling-down vats then gone back to the saloon and eaten his share of supper.'

Her look was disapproving but there was a reluctant touch of admiration there, too.

This 'kid' was turning out to be one tough *hombre*.

CHAPTER 5

BULLETS & HEADSTONES

Dusty directed Craig to the livery and when he stopped the buckboard at the double doors, climbed down.

'I have to go see my lawyer about Dad's will. It will take some time so I may stop over in town tonight. If I do finish early I'll hire a horse and ride out. Meantime, I'd like you to get Dad's headstone set up. Price will show you where – he has cement and the rest of what you'll need.'

She paused and looked at him dabbing at a still-bleeding cut on his face. 'If you feel you need to see the doctor, I'm willing to pay the bill.'

He smiled crookedly. 'Ain't you got the picture yet? I'm a big tough bucko who's been round Cape Horn four times.' At her frown – obviously she wasn't sure if he was boasting or jesting – he added, 'No, I'm fine, Dusty. I'll be stiff and sore but that's to be expected. I could wait around if you'd rather ride back in the buckboard?'

No. it was settled: she would see the lawyer and make her own way back. She waved and walked across the street to a line of buildings with signs on their doorways.

Fargo turned the team over to the livery man to rub down and feed while he washed up in a nearby rain barrel. The livery man, grey-haired and looking to be in his seventies, called one of his helpers to do the chore, then went to the buckboard tray and studied the headstone.

'Gonna miss ol' George. See that stone? Ribbed red marble. Jonas Tate, the stonemason, had to send all the way to Denver for that slab, but it was George's favourite stone and Dusty wouldn't have it any other way.'

Wiping his face on a cloth the livery man handed him, Fargo nodded at the carved dates: 1806-1881. 'Didn't realize George was so old.'

'Yeah. Married late, woman in her forties – she died birthin' Dusty. Lonely man, George: used to come in once a week with a jug of sourmash and we'd swap yarns. Gonna miss him.'

'Couple of old soldiers reminiscing, huh?'

'Hell, no. *I* was too old for the war and George only had one leg – well, one and a half, off just below the knee. Lost it years ago when he was building his big dam.'

Fargo shook his head slowly. 'I didn't know that. I dunno why, but I thought he'd been in the army.'

And if he hadn't, how did he know Morgan Fargo? Or any of the others on the list. . . ?

Bascombe was a mess. His face was swollen, badly cut and bruised, welts showing where the layers of rope had punished him, eyes puffy, the left one almost closed. His nostrils were clogged with congealed blood, his nose puffed-up, with a decidedly starboard lean.

In the saloon, he stood alone at one end of the counter. The big shambling barkeep took pity on him, poured him a double whiskey, growling, 'On the house – somethin' I never thought I'd ever say to you, Bascombe. But, man, you are so *miserable-lookin'* it fair tugs at my heart strings.'

Other drinkers nearby chuckled, staring at the big, battered man. He was not popular, but he leered briefly and sipped the whiskey – his lips were too split and puffy for him to toss it down fast.

'That Craig better not figure he's heard the last of me!' he grated.

No one said anything, leaving him alone with his miseries. *They all knew Bascombe's capacity for revenge: sneaky, and very, very brutal – dark alleys preferred. . . .*

Then a man who had been sitting at a corner table sauntered across, casually adjusting his slanting gunbelt, the holstered Colt on his left thigh. He was slim, under six feet, and sported a blond moustache which matched his hair that showed under the narrow-brimmed hat. His face was triangular; what could be seen of the mouth full enough but with a down-turn at the corners. He leaned on the bar alongside Bascombe who glanced up, glaring at the stranger.

The man gestured to the almost empty glass. 'Want another? You look like you could use it.'

Bascombe started to snarl but the chance of free drinks stopped him. He nodded curtly, then winced and grabbed at his bruised neck.

'Done you over good, didn't he?' the stranger said gesturing at the barkeep to refill Bascombe's glass. He slid a coin across the counter. 'I'll take a shot, too. Bring 'em over to the table.'

He nudged Bascombe's arm and gestured to the table he had left earlier, walking on ahead. A little warily, Bascombe drained his glass and limped after him. He sat down heavily in a straightback chair and said in his raspy voice, 'What you want with me?'

The man lifted a finger and said nothing until after the drinks had been set before them.

'Who are you?' Bascombe asked. 'I seen you before – 'bout a month ago, here in town.'

'Yeah, had some business then. Just passing back through. Name's Al. I seen you get your facial massage out there earlier.'

Bascombe scowled, picked up his glass and sipped half of it. 'Thanks for the drink, but I ain't about to tell you what it feels like to get shellacked with a coiled rope.'

'Now you know how the hosses you've used one on feel.'

Bascombe frowned, wincing again as blood oozed

from the cut he had earned at Fargo's hands out at Slash S. 'Listen, what the hell d'you want?'

'Aw, mebbe I feel kinda sorry for you, taking that beating. It'd have most men dragging their tails off to some hidey-hole where they could lay in their misery and cuss-out the sonuver who done it to 'em – and mebbe plan how they was gonna get even.'

For the first time, Bascombe noticed the chill in the blue eyes, like chips of ice. He felt a little uneasy but didn't know why, so he just shrugged. 'I'll square things in my own time.'

'Sure, don't blame you. . . . Did I hear you call that kid "Craig"?' At the sudden switch, Bascombe blinked, then nodded. 'That his first or last name?'

'Hell, I dunno. I just heard that bitch from Slash S call him Craig. Why? You think you know him?'

Al pushed his glass across to Bascombe. 'You need this more'n me. Go ahead, I can order more if you want, but first you got to tell me how bad you want to square things with this Craig.'

'*How bad?* Judas, mister, how bad you *think*! I want to kill the son of a bitch!'

Al's full lips moved in a strange sort of smile, like the muscles were rippling along the length of the upper lip, right to left. . . .

'Figured you might,' he said and lifted a hand to catch the barkeep's eye. 'Make it mighty sweet if you was paid somethin' as well, huh?'

It would be sundown before Craig Fargo was finished setting the headstone in place.

The grave was next to another, much older one, bordered with carefully matched stones, of a shape and size that gave a neat finishing touch to outlining the grave area. A smaller tombstone – also made of ribbed red marble – sat at the head, canted slightly off the vertical so the carving could be read more easily:

Martha Sloane. Beloved Wife of George. Sadly missed. The information was followed by a set of dates, the latter being about twenty-five years earlier. . . .

Price had told him she was a frail woman. George had fallen for her and was badly cut up when she died. So much so that for the first few years of Dusty's life he paid little attention to her, hired town women to rear her.

Then one day he seemed to come to his senses and realized it was not *her* fault Martha had died. That if anyone could be blamed it should be him.

From then on he had lavished plenty of love, both paternally and materially, on the girl. But she had shown her mother's stubbornness and independence and while it was obvious she loved her father, they had plenty of clashes. But Slash S prospered and as the years passed the hostility dwindled.

'Livery man was telling me George had only one leg.'

'Yeah, used too much dynamite to blast down a rock wall. Never slowed him much, though. Sent away East to someplace that made him a contraption of leather and steel braces and he stomped about pretty good. Couldn't fight when the war came but did his bit for the Confederacy by supplyin' 'em with cattle and horses for low prices. Towards the end when their funds ran out, he just told 'em to take what they wanted.'

'I guess that's one way of fightin' a war.'

'Hell, the Sloanes did more'n their bit. George's two brothers went to the fightin', too. One got killed and t'other spent years in a Yankee prison camp. Come out, well, some folk, say not quite right in the head. No, no one can say the Sloanes din' do their part for the South.'

Now, the cement mixed and some poured into the shallow hole, Fargo washed over the headstone while it settled some, then muscled the heavy slab of marble across. His shoulders creaked as he wrapped his arms about it and lowered it into the hole, its own weight sinking it several inches deep into the still-wet cement.

He fiddled about with rocks and sticks, angling it back to the approximate slant of Martha's tombstone, propping it into position. Then he mixed the rest of the cement and poured it around the base, troweling it smooth after tamping it down.

He glanced at the sky-fire in the west. Clouds started to glow as the sun sank, outlining the hills, and it flashed off something up in the rocks of the slope overlooking the small graveyard.

Instinctively, Craig dropped flat and an instant later something *thunked*! into the edge of George's headstone and whined away viciously, marble chips stinging his left side.

He recognized the snarl and whine of a ricocheting bullet.

He rolled swiftly in between the grave mounds and dirt spattered him as another three vicious, swiftly fired bullets sought him. He had no six-gun but Dusty had given him a Winchester to keep with him when riding the range, in case of wolves and other predators. He reckoned that included human ones.

The rifle was in the tray of the buckboard which stood a few feet away, the tailgate still lowered. As yet another shot came his way, stirring the air close to his face this time, he lunged for the rear of the buckboard.

The team was nervous with the gunfire echoing down from the hills and the bullets thudding so close. They jerked forward as he lunged for the tailgate. He saw it going out of reach, made a mighty effort and launched himself in a dive. His fingers caught the ridge where the tailgate fitted at its base and he clawed desperately, legs trailing out from under him, boots scrabbling wildly.

He got a grip and with a loud grunt of effort, scrambled into the heaving tray. He rolled right across, hitting his head hard against the side. But he grabbed the rifle and slid around even as he levered a shell into the breech. The team started to run now and the buckboard swayed and bumped over the rough ground, throwing him around roughly. Splinters flew as another shot from the hidden gunman chewed an edge off the tailgate. He rolled on to his back, slid and lost his grip as he tried to grab the wood. It was no good! He would never be able to shoot under these conditions – he would only be wasting ammunition.

So he rolled to the tailgate as the team turned down the slope and dropped off the edge. He hit the pile of dirt he had dug out to make the hole for the headstone and it broke his fall somewhat and also provided him with a barely adquate shelter from the bushwacker.

He rolled quickly on to his belly, sore muscles protesting. There was plenty of gunsmoke drifting up out of a pile of rocks on the hillside to give him the shooter's rough position. He even saw a blurred movement as the man became impatient at his bad shooting and lifted up behind his shelter. Fargo triggered and the man dropped instantly. He saw the tip of a battered hat moving fast behind a low rock as the killer shifted posiiton.

With one raking glance with eyes that could pick up the ripples of a sounding whale a mile across a sunglaring sea, he saw where he figured the man would be making fore: a low breastwork of shale with two stunted bushes in front. Good cover, but Fargo had noticed this when driving down-slope to where the graveyard was and he knew he was slightly higher.

To make sure, he got his legs under him and ran, crouching, up the slope and dropped behind a deadfall just as the other man reached his cover. Within seconds the killer was shooting at where he had last seen Fargo, then reared back as stone chips stung his face when two bullets thudded into the shale that protected him. He got such a shock he fell and half rolled on to his back as he levered desperately, struggling to get back to a shooting position.

Fargo fired again from his raised position and the bullet shattered the man's left shoulder spinning him violently. He screamed. His face came around as Fargo got him in his sights once more.

The man's identity was no real surprise: it was Bascombe.

Reluctantly, Fargo held his fire.

He took the badly wounded man to Slash S headquarters in the back of the buckboard. At first, Bascombe yelled and cussed like a trooper in the last stages of combat fatigue, and then his voice dwindled away into a series of mumbles so that by the time the Slash S crew came out of the lantern-lit bunkhouse, he was unconscious,

'Judas, you surely are givin' Bascombe a taste of his own medicine!' opined Satterlee while Lockie Bruce nodded.

'He'd better have some first aid or he'll bleed to death,' Price said. 'But I gotta say I'm reluctant to do anythin' to help this back-shootin' bastard.'

The attention to the wound, with its shattered bone visible through mangled flesh, brought yells and obscenities from Bascombe and while he rallied once or twice, raging briefly, he fell back in a dead faint as Price finished tying-off the rough bandages.

'Poley,' Price said to one of the cowhands, 'You can take him in to Doc Melrose.' Poley groaned but Price held up a hand, and continued: 'You'd be goin' in to pick up that barbed wire in the mornin', anyway. Take Bascombe in now, leave him at the sawbones, then stay over till Halliday opens his store in the mornin' – if you want the chore, of course.'

'Hell I'll do it!' Poley turned back towards the bunkhouse: the prospect of a night in town appealed. . . .

'There's one other thing,' Lockie Bruce said, grabbing their attention. He held up a small wad of paper money. 'This was in Bascombe's pocket, just short of fifty bucks. Could be it was fifty and he stopped for a bracer or two before comin' out to drygulch you, Craig.'

'Someone paid him to nail me?' Fargo looked and sounded surprised. 'Hell, the picture I got of Bascombe he was a low, vindictive snake. I was even expecting him to make a try for me. He wouldn't need to be paid.'

Satterlee looked down at the injured man and shook his head. 'But if someone offered, he sure wouldn't say no.'

Price looked sharply at Fargo. 'You got enemies in Rio Blanco?'

'I figure it'd be someone who'd want to stop me searching, but I wasn't expectin' anything to happen so soon.'

'George was the last one, wasn't he? I mean there is one more but you can't even make out his name or anythin' about him, so I guess he's safe.'

'Mightn't necessarily *feel* safe,' Fargo said.

'If you're right,' Price said slowly,' it means someone's trailed you here.'

Fargo nodded, looking down at the unconscious

Bascombe. 'Mebbe I better take him into the saw-bones. Sure would like to be there when he comes to.'

Poley looked mighty disappointed and Craig Fargo savvied how the man must feel. 'I'll stand nighthawk for you when you're due next, Poley. It's mighty important I find out if someone paid Bascombe to come after me.'

Poley brightened. 'You got a deal, mister!'

'OK, you can bring Dusty back with you tomorrow,' Price said. 'She usually stays with Widow Franklin – got a roomin' house on Dallas Street. You can't miss it.'

Craig found it easily enough after leaving Bascombe – still out of his head with pain – at the doctor's.

The sawbones had examined the wounded man and sighed. He was a middle-aged man with a heavy tobacco-stained moustache.

'I really don't feel like doing anything to help such a blackguard as Bascombe . . . God forgive me.'

'He sure ain't on anyone's popularity lists around here.'

'Well, I'll do what I can, I suppose. I've given my sacred oath to do that – for all and sundry.'

'When can I talk with him, Doc?'

'With the amount of cholorform I'll have to give him and the time it'll take me to operate, not until tomorrow.'

Disappointed, Fargo left and went to the rooming house Price had told him about.

The rather intimidating Widow Franklin gave him a close going-over, both visually and with biting questions.

But Dusty heard the voices, looked out and came to Fargo's rescue.

'It's all right, Mrs Franklin. Craig works for me.'

'I'll be in my parlour should you need me,' the widow said with a final raking glare at Fargo.

Dusty smiled as the door closed behind her.

'She's like a mother hen. I don't know if you noticed the sign. . . ?' She gestured to the shingle swinging on its slim chain above the porch where they stood.

'I did notice the "Ladies Of Good Repute Only" sign,' Fargo admitted with a crooked smile. Then he explained briefly why he was in town. Dusty frowned.

'It does sound as if Bascombe was hired to shoot you – not that he would need the extra incentive.'

'That's what I reckoned. I'll see what I can pick up at the saloon. Price figured you could come back to Slash S with me in the buckboard.'

Dusty agreed and as Fargo turned away, she placed a hand on his arm. 'Be careful, Craig – asking if someone hired an assassin could get you in trouble.'

'There a sheriff in town?'

'Yes, Win Braden. I think you'd better tell him what's happened.'

'*After* I talk to Bascombe.'

'That might not be such a good idea. The sheriff is a mite – touchy. I expect you don't need any more trouble.'

He smiled wryly, and touched a hand to his hatbrim.

'I've about had my fill of it these last eight years,' he admitted. 'I'll see Braden, but, like I said, *after* I've talked with Bascombe.'

Her teeth tugged at her bottom lip as he walked away, the rifle slanting from his left hand.

CHAPTER 6

'NO GUNS IN TOWN'

Fargo entered the saloon, carrying his rifle easily.

The barroom was like almost every other saloon he had seen in ports around the world as well as the American West – smoke-heavy, a babble of voices, an occasional sound of breaking glass as booze-clumsy hands dropped or knocked over a bottle. A few voices raised in argument. Dice rattled and cards were shuffled.

The barkeep was big, wore a collarless shirt and rolls of neck fat bulged over it. He was called 'Babe'.

'No naked guns in here, mister.' He held out a big hand. 'I'll look after it for you.'

His eyes were hard and his other hand was below the counter top. Fargo hesitated, then smiled thinly and pushed the rifle across. 'Keep it handy.'

The barkeep's eyes narrowed. 'I'll give it back when you're leavin'.'

Craig shrugged, took out a coin from his vest pocket – Dusty had been thoughtful enough to advance him a few dollars against his pay. 'Beer.'

As Babe drew it and set the foaming glass down, Fargo asked, 'Bascombe in here earlier?'

'He was.'

'He tried to drygulch me out at Slash S just on sundown.' The 'keep's eyes narrowed and a couple of other drinkers with their ears hanging out to catch the talk stiffened. 'He had the best part of fifty bucks in his pocket. From what I hear, he mostly bummed drinks or rolled a drunk when he needed cash.'

'You heard right – I wouldn't know how he come by that much money.'

Fargo let his look linger, then turned casually, elbow on the counter edge. 'How about you fellers?'

The eavesdroppers shook their heads, but he noticed they both looked past his shoulder first. Sipping his beer he turned slowly and saw card players and gamblers at a row of tables – and, nearer, a man with a blond moustache sitting alone, chair turned slightly so he could see the bar. He was staring at Fargo whose voice would have easily carried that far.

The blond man said nothing, but lifted his shotglass and drank slowly, keeping his cool blue gaze on Fargo, who turned and drained his beer.

Fargo walked across to the table where the blond man sat, watching him carefully. He noticed the man wore his six-gun low on his left side, holster base tied down. He touched the back of an empty chair. 'You mind?'

'Yeah, I mind – I don't want company.' The man stiffened as Fargo sat down anyway. 'Listen! I just said—'

'You don't want company. I heard. Name's Craig Fargo.' The blue eyes flickered although the man shrugged.

'So? I seen you beat the hell outta some feller this afternoon outside there, but I ain't buying you no drinks.'

'You hear me tell the 'keep that feller tried to back-shoot me?' The blond man showed no interest. 'He was carrying just short of fifty bucks. Kinda looked like someone might've paid him to take a shot at me.'

'I still ain't interested and if you don't get outta that chair and leave me alone I'll take a shot at you.'

Fargo smiled slightly and spread his hands. 'Barkeep's got my gun.'

The blond man flicked his gaze briefly to the gawkers at the bar. 'Anyone want to lend him a six-gun?'

The drinkers stiffened. The barkeep jerked his head at his helper, mouthing the word 'sheriff', then licked his lips, as the man slid out the rear door. He said tersely to the blond man, 'No gunplay in here, mister.'

The blond man pinned him with his cold eyes. 'You want to buy in?'

'Hell, no! Listen, I know who your are, Bisby. You got a reputation, even down here.' He paused and

Fargo could see that Bisby liked what the man had said.

'You're *Al Bisby*!'

'You heard about me, too, huh?'

Fargo nodded gently. 'Heard some things. I'm no gunfighter – I'm not gonna go up against you.'

'Yaller?'

'Mebbe I'm just not stupid enough to try to outdraw a man with your reputation.'

All this talk about 'reputation' seemed to please Bisby. 'Well, you need to watch your mouth, mister, comin' in here and accusing me of hirin' Bascombe to bushwack you.'

'Is that what I did?' Fargo asked innocently.

'Hell, way you beat him, he wouldn't need to be paid to square with you! He'd bust a gut to do it.'

'Sure, and it'd look exactly right if he *did* do it, wouldn't it, after our fight? If anyone offered him fifty bucks, why, that'd be just added incentive.'

Al Bisby was on his feet now, left hand hovering above his gunbutt. 'You better get yourself a gun!'

'Told you, I'm no good with a six-gun. How about axes?'

Bisby blinked. 'Axes! The hell you talkin' about?'

'See who can cut down a tree the fastest – then make it fall just where you want.'

Bisby was very tense now. His jaw was working so that his moustache seemed to rock above his mouth. 'You got a deathwish!' He snapped at the barman. 'You! Give him that six-gun you keep under the bar! Come on! *Give it to him!*'

Babe shook his head just as the batwings slapped open and a tall man with a polished brass star pinned to his shirt pocket stepped swiftly into the barroom: the local law, carrying a sawn-off shotgun, raked wild eyes in a sweating face around the room.

'What's goin' on here?' He picked out the gunfighter immediately, saw Fargo was unarmed and jerked the shotgun at Bisby. 'Forget it, mister! No shooting in my town – unless I do it.'

Al Bisby smiled crookedly, his left hand still hovering over his gunbutt. 'Well. . . ?' *Was that a challenge?*

'My gun's cocked!' warned the sheriff, a little wildly and Fargo knew the lawman was afraid of this Bisby but was stubbornly going to do what he saw as his duty.

'I could nail you before the fall of the hammer,' Bisby said confidently, and as Sheriff Braden suddenly changed his grip on the shotgun with one of his sweating hands, Bisby's gun came up, blazing.

Braden reeled and twisted away with the strike of the bullet. His shotgun thundered, the charge punching out a panel in the bar front. Some of the buckshot hit Babe in the legs and the big man groaned as he fell to his knees.

The shotgun clattered as the sheriff fell face down in the sawdust. A man at the bar ran for the door. Other drinkers dived for cover.

Fargo dropped to the floor as the smoking pistol turned in his direction. Then something prodded him in the ribs and he looked around sharply: the downed barkeep was thrusting his rifle at him through the ragged hole blasted in the bar front panel, even as

Bisby said, 'That was a fair shoot-out. Everyone seen he was goin' to shoot but I was just too fast.' Smirking, he looked around almost as if he was expecting someone to cheer, then returned his gaze to Fargo. 'Guess you're still backin' down?'

'Like I said, I'd be a damn fool to go up against someone as fast as you with a six-gun, but. . . .' He levered a shell into the rifle's breech and Bisby, startled, triggered, taken off-guard by Fargo's action.

The bullet thudded into the bar front as Fargo fired the rifle one-handed, his shot going wild into a wall. The gunfighter laughed, bringing up his smoking pistol again, 'I ain't finished with you, mister!'

Fargo levered again, his hand a blur, shot instantly, and Bisby's hat spun off his head. Completely startled, head bleeding, the gunfighter lurched violently. He had been thrown in the direction of the rear door, and staggered the extra couple of feet, shooting once more without even looking back at Fargo, as he lurched out into the night.

It was clear Al Bisby was *not* used to his targets shooting back.

A man picked up the bullet-torn hat and said, 'Hey, you almost nailed him, feller! There's blood on this hat.'

' "Almost" might not be good enough,' Fargo said quietly.

He knew how close he had just come to dying.

Sheriff Win Braden was a lucky man; Bisby's bullet had struck his heavy brass star, punched almost through the metal and damaged the chest muscle on that side. He was in a great deal of pain so the doctor sedated him.

While the sawbones was drying his hands, Fargo asked, 'How about Bascombe, Doc?'

'A good question. He'll probably live, being the kind of mean hardcase he is. He won't be conscious until sometime tomorrow, though.'

'He say anything while he was under the chloroform?'

The medic looked at him sharply. 'How d'you know about such things?'

'I read a medical book on the whaler, they figured that was good enough to make me ship's "doctor".'

'Huh! Well, he did murmur a couple of times about "Al". Kept saying he wanted his money. He could have been talking about the fifty dollars.'

'Sounds like it. Well, thanks, Doc. I'd better go see if the livery man will let me use his loft for tonight.'

As Fargo turned away the doctor said, 'Young man, you would do well to sleep with one eye open. Al Bisby is not someone to accept that you creased his head and drove him out of that saloon.' At Fargo's quizzical look, he added, 'I have worked in other towns where he plied his trade. Enough dollars would always buy his gun. But to make sure of that, he has to live up to his reputation.'

'Thanks, Doc. I'll sleep with my rifle.'

'Er, why did you take a headshot? His body would have made an easier target.'

'Didn't want to kill him. Need to have a few words

with him. Anyway, I'm used to headshots.' At the saw-bones' startled reaction, Fargo smiled. 'When they had me on that ship, we did a season of sealing – filthy, bloody work on freezing, barren islands on the under-belly of Australia. A place called Bass Strait, but locals reckon it's "straight from hell" – because of the bad storms, I guess. Usually the sealers beat the animals' brains out; you'd be surprised at how many of the bas-tards get to like it – pummellin' and pulpin' unnecessarily. I took a rifle and shot the seals in the head, to put 'em outta their misery.'

'You are a very interesting young man, Mr Fargo.'

'And hope to grow into a very interesting *old* man. . . . Mebbe I'll write a book about it someday, Doc.'

Fargo spent the night in the livery's loft with his rifle under his blanket but there was no sign of Al Bisby.

Next morning he picked up Dusty Sloane at the rooming house.

She settled beside him in the driving seat of the buckboard and, apart from a courteous 'Good morning', didn't speak again until they were climbing the plateau to the high country where Slash S sprawled.

'I heard about the shooting in the saloon.' He said nothing as she dropped the words suddenly. 'You – you are a surprising young man, Craig Fargo.'

'Interestin', too, according to Doc.' He grinned when he spoke. 'I'd've liked to've had a talk with Bisby.'

'You think he killed Dad with that tree, like Price claims?'

'Almost certainly. He's a southpaw for a start. Anyway, from what Doc said, I think he'll hang around. He'll want to kill me if he can.' At her surprised look, he added, 'He can't be sure how much my father told me and if he's been hired by someone to kill off the men on Pa's list. . . .'

'I see. You don't sound very worried.'

'It just don't show, is all.'

'Have you any notion at all what it may be about?'

'Not really. Something that happened in the war, I guess. They all seem to have known each other there. Must've been in the same squad, or something. . . .'

'Except for Dad.'

'Yeah, that's the puzzler. He's the odd man out. Not likely he knew those fellers if he wasn't actually in the war, but he must've had some connection with 'em or he wouldn't've been on the list. Er, would he have any papers that might throw a light on it?'

'I went through his things, of course, but I never came across anything. The only connection with the war was his sales of beef and remounts to the Confederacy. He was very loyal to the South. You're welcome to look through his things, though, if you want.'

He accepted gladly: he had to get more of a hold on this. Six men had died already. *He* was on Bisby's kill-list, too. There had to be some common link.

Had to be. . . .

'I wonder why they suddenly raided your father's

place? I mean the war had been over for years. . . .'

'Been giving it some thought. Maybe whoever's behind it was gettin' ready for some sort of big deal and if it got out, or even hinted at, that those men had any connection with—' He shrugged. 'I dunno, some deal that went wrong, maybe, or a secret raid they didn't want made public, even after all these years.'

She nodded. 'I see. It could ruin their chances of doing whatever was being planned. Ye-es. That sounds possible. Start getting rid of survivors in case something was leaked.' She smiled wryly. 'It does sound like a long shot, though, doesn't it?'

'Haven't come up with anything better yet – and it's a long time since they killed Pa. . . .'

She frowned. 'Yes! That is strange.'

The whole damn thing is strange, he thought. *Strange, but deadly!*

CHAPTER 7

WRONG MAN

After leaving the girl at the ranch – and noting how quiet she was on the ride home, memories stirring, no doubt – Fargo gathered some tools and went back to the grave site.

Here he re-set George Sloane's headstone: it had been knocked out of kilter during the gunfight with Bascombe and had a decided lean to it. He chipped away at the cement with cold chisel and hammer, mixed more and set the stone squarely in position. It didn't move when he gave it a good shake so he got down on hands and knees, and, to his surprise, found most of the chips of red marble that had been chewed out of the rear edge by Bascombe's bullet on the right hand side of the headstone.

He'd asked the Mexican cook for an old coffee strainer and he mixed more cement and laboriously forced a small amount through the sieve several times, taking out the grit and leaving a tolerably smooth paste. He used this to stick in the chips of marble where they fitted, wiping each join carefully with a wet cloth.

It wasn't perfect, for there were a few small pieces still missing, but he reckoned it was better than before.

He felt for Dusty – she had been holding back the tears with a true effort on the last part of the run back from town. He guessed that the session with the lawyer and going over the will had likely stirred many memories. She had hurried into the house on arrival at the ranch and had merely waved when he had said he would go check the headstone.

Now, satisfied it was the best he could do, Fargo gathered his tools and went back to the ranch.

She was in the parlour, bright with afternoon sun, and working at embroidering a large multi-coloured quilt, which spilled across her lap, folds dragging on the floor. She glanced up and gave him a quick smile, ducking her head again over the embroidery she was working on.

He saw many images that marked it most definitely as being a memorabilia quilt, dedicated to the South. Making such quilts was popular with women who were adept with needle and thread, even so long after the war. He was amazed at the amount of work that must have gone into it.

Quietly he told her about repairing the headstone and she looked up, not trying to hide her reddened eyes now.

'That was thoughtful of you, Craig, and I thank you.

I may leave it until tomorrow before I go to look at your handiwork.' Again the quick on-off smile. 'You'll understand I've had an . . . upsetting time these last couple of days with a lot of memories stirred.'

'Sure. I just hope the stone is to your liking.' He gestured to the quilt: it had to be a labour of love. 'You must've put in some long hours on that.'

'This is the second year.' She smiled as his eyebrows arched in surprise. 'I – I was making it for Dad's seventy-fifth birthday. Gathered some memories for him and put them together here in embroidery. See this pinto pony? That was my seventh birthday gift. And here? The wishing well? I'd heard him say he wished he had two legs so he could fight the Yankees, so I dug a small hole, filled it with water and made a little roof over it with part of a broken doll's house my Uncle Gary had made for me. So then he had the ranch-hands dig a proper full-size well and called it *Dusty's Desire*. And the old barn on this block was the one he built for us to live in while he and my uncles got on with the ranch, and. . . .'

She went on and on and he didn't interrupt, sensing that this was good for her, easing the grief she must still be feeling. She brightened considerably.

Then as she moved the folds to show him an elaborate scene with a man holding a rifle beside an alert-looking hunting dog by a wooded lake, he saw the names, *Caleb and Gary Sloane*, on the block next to it, which depicted two soldiers in Confederate uniforms. One was shorter than the other, wearing a black kepi cap, while the tall man had the more normal grey.

'Why the different caps?'

She sobered and ran a hand lightly over the panel. 'My uncles – Caleb is the one in the black cap: he was killed in battle south of the Missouri Breaks early in the war. The other one is, of course, Uncle Gary.'

'He's the one who survived the prison camp?'

'Yes. He had a dreadful ordeal. Apparently they wanted some particular information they believed he had and, well, he resisted their worst torture. He's a haunted man to this day.' Her voice trailed off and Fargo thought her eyes were beginning to fill again, but she swallowed and lifted her head, making an effort to fight returning memories. 'He managed to escape the prison camp but almost died doing it. Some Indians found him and nursed him until he was fit enough to come back – less of a man after the way he had been treated. He was unable to face life, I suppose. Didn't care for human company and eventually went away to live a solitary life up in the Otero Mountains. He built himself a small place up there, a sort of trading post, and called it "Restoration". It's primarily for the use of Indians: he's never forgotten how they saved his life.'

'You're still in touch then?'

She frowned slightly at his sudden animation. 'Well, yes and no. He sends me a birthday card each year, always postmarked at Barnabas, a kind of off-beat Indian agency at the foot of the range. I write and thank him, care of the agency, but he never replies . . . just sends another card on my next birthday.'

He straightened. 'How long since your last one?'

'About eight months – almost nine . . . why?'

Fargo's hands balled into fists. 'Then you don't know for sure if he is still alive?'

She stiffened. 'Oh, I would hope so! He didn't have any kind of a deathwish, just wanted the solitude, and Dad said we ought to respect that.' Her frown deepened. 'I can understand why you'd like to see him, his having been in the army and all, but I have a feeling there's something more to it than that. . . ?'

Fargo was silent for a spell then he heaved a sigh and said, 'His name's Gary, right? Initial "G", same as "G" for "George", your father's name?'

'Ye-es, but—'

'Dusty, Pa had just written "G. Sloane, Dixon County" on the paper. If Bisby found there was a G. Sloane running a ranch right here in the county, he'd've figured he had the man he wanted, right?'

Her hand went' quickly to her mouth. 'Oh my God! You're saying . . . Bisby killed the wrong man!'

'I think that's the only answer, Dusty. And I think we have to go find your Uncle Gary as soon as possible before Bisby realizes his mistake.'

Al Bisby had a headache that beat the worst hangover he'd ever had – and it was growing worse.

He knew what it was: not so much that the bullet crease was getting any more serious, but wholly and solely *because he had been beaten*! Judas Priest, it hadn't happened to him in a coon's age – he couldn't remember when. (And didn't want to!) He was feeling low enough already.

77

That damn Fargo: helluva surprise. Looks like just a tough kid – and he *is* tough – and *fast*! It had shaken Bisby badly coming out on the wrong end of a shoot-out and he had taken to the hills, rested up in a sulk, which didn't help his throbbing head any.

He had the shallow wound covered with a bandanna he had tied around his head, but was still hatless. Didn't feel quite right, no hat. . . .

But there were things to do, *important* things that had to take precedence over his physical comfort. There was that mean-assed throwback, Bascombe, for one thing. *One damn important* thing: he must've been out of his head hiring a fool like that to take care of Fargo. It had seemed like a good idea at the time: Bascombe had been beaten up by Fargo and was unforgiving, so he was the logical one to suspect should Fargo turn up with a bullet in the back, or, seeing as Bascombe was the one pulling the trigger, maybe in the belly. But the fool had muffed it and now was like something dragged out from under a runaway locomotive. *May he suffer hugely!*

But he was likely to talk if it would get him relief from his pain. Like all cowards, pain was not one of the things a bully like Bascombe could endure – he could only dish it out.

So . . . now he had to risk his neck and go shut Bacombe's mouth for keeps.

It was not a good start, for he was afoot and couldn't go near the livery to get his mount. He knew he had winged the sheriff, but Braden was known to be tough and would likely have men looking for him. He didn't think the lawman was hit badly enough to be kept in Doc Melrose's infirmary so would probably join in the manhunt himself.

Yeah! So he figured it would be safe to get to Bascombe at the infirmary. He didn't want to have to kill the sawbones – doctors were too damn popular in these one-horse towns – but he wouldn't hesitate if he got in the way.

He knew *he* wouldn't last long if it got back to The Boss that he had let Fargo live, not knowing how much the kid's father had told him. . . .

He was keeping to the shadows as he approached the doctor's house when suddenly the door opened and light spilled out, throwing moving shadows across the porch.

'Well, smoke me!' Bisby said half aloud as he hunkered down against a fence, left hand holding his six-gun. 'Now, ain't that convenient!'

There were three men at the doorway: Doc Melrose, Sheriff Braden – and Bascombe! The latter looked sick, one arm in a sling, but the lawman held his good arm firmly. Some of his words to the medic came clearly to Bisby:

'I'm all through arguin', Doc! Bascombe tried to kill that feller Fargo and his place is in jail.'

'For God's sake, Sheriff! The man's half dead! He's not even fully recovered from the operation.'

'He'll have a cell to himself, Doc. Feel free to come visit anytime you like.'

'You haven't heard the last of this! Bascombe is not one of my favourite patients, but I'm sworn to help *anyone* who needs my ministrations and—'

'I ain't stoppin' you, Doc. I told you, come visit him anytime. *But he's goin' in the cells*! G'night to you.'

Braden half dragged the no-doubt moaning Bascombe down the short set of steps and after calling the lawman a couple of times, the medic slammed the door angrily.

Bisby smiled crookedly, checking his Colt's cylinder. He was about to step out and blast both men stumbling away towards the law office, but held his fire, even holstered the gun. There were still folk on the streets enjoying the balmy evening, and, being a man who liked an audience, Bisby stopped, spread his boots firmly and worked the fingers of his left hand before holding it above his gun.

'Hey, Braden! How about it? Feelin' lucky?'

The sheriff stumbled slightly as he spun about, still trying to steady the semi-conscious Bascombe. He squinted, at first not recognizing Bisby, but then he did, and saw his left hand's fingers wriggling as the man kept them supple for the draw. Some folk nearby had heard and stopped to stare.

'You're crazy, Bisby! You kill a lawman and—'

'And nothin'! I got all the protection I need. Now, you gonna draw? Or just stand there an' die?'

Braden let Bascombe fall, leaping aside in an attempt to divert Bisby's concentration, hand sweeping back to his gunbutt. He staggered as Bisby's Colt smashed two shots into his chest, his gun falling to the dust. In moments, he had joined it, one arm outflung arm across the twitching legs of the moaning Bascombe.

Grinning tightly, aware the startled townsfolk were already coming closer to see what had happened, Bisby walked up to Bascombe and, standing over him, lowered his smoking gun barrel to within three inches of the man's head.

He fired. This action scattered the townsfolk and he started to turn away, but then he paused to reach back and pick up Sheriff Braden's hat which had rolled off.

He jammed it on his head as he sprinted for the nearest hitchrail and slapped loose the reins of the horse tethered there.

He quit town at a gallop, the outraged cowboy owner of the horse bawling curses as he sprinted after him.

While Fargo was strapping the supplies on the pack-horse, which stood patiently, nose buried in a bag with a handful of oats, he heard a horse coming into the ranch yard at a fast clip.

It was the long-faced outrider, Poley. He skidded his mount to a halt outside the barn, leaping from the saddle.

'You're in a hurry. Enjoy your night on the town?'

'Damn right! You'll be sorry you missed out.'

'I've had nights on the town before.'

'Not like this!' Poley swaggered across to stand closer, grinning tightly. 'That gunfighter – Bisby. He out-drew the sheriff an' killed Bascombe while he lay on the ground! Stole a hoss and left 'em both dead in the middle of Main.'

Fargo stiffened, listening as the excited Poley went

into detail. His loud talk brought other cowhands to the door of the nearby bunkhouse and, basking in the attention, he started at the beginning for those who hadn't heard it all.

Fargo finished tightening the load and hurried into the house where Dusty was checking through her bedroll.

'I have to tell you – Al Bisby's still about.'

She jerked her head up. 'Here?'

He told her quickly what Poley had said, adding, 'I figure he'll be dogging us all the way to the Oteros.'

'As long as that's all he does!'

'I think we'll be safe enough – until he's sure of where we're going, anyway. I reckon he's realized he killed the wrong man now and aims to set things to rights.'

Some of the colour drained from Dusty's face. 'I'll get you a six-gun to go with your rifle. And I think I'd better get one for myself.'

'Might be wise,' Fargo said shortly. 'Unless you want to give me directions to the Indian agency and I can find your uncle and—'

'No! Go saddle my horse, Craig! I'll get the guns. *Both* of us are riding into those mountains.'

As he nodded and went out into the yard, she murmured to herself, 'I just hope both of us are going to ride out of those mountains, too.'

CHAPTER 8

NIGHT TRAIL

They started out before sunup, figuring it wasn't likely Al Bisby was watching the ranch from close enough to see them slip away in the dark. They did not light lanterns. Before turning in they placed everything they needed where they could easily find it again in the dark.

Lockie Bruce was going with them as a backup through the rugged country they needed to cross. He claimed to know it pretty well. Price, foreman and a veteran employee of Slash S, was left in charge of the ranch.

There was no moon to speak of at the time they left and the stars were fading. Price came to see them off, helping with the packhorses which Fargo had offloaded the night before.

'Dusty,' Price said quietly, 'can't you alert Gary in some way?'

'He's isolated up in those mountains. His trading post stands alone, so they tell me. There's no nearby town.'

'How about the Indian agency where he sends your birthday cards from?' Fargo said. 'If they have a telegraph they could send a man out to Gary and put him on his guard.'

Dusty nodded. 'That's an idea! I'm not sure about the agency having a telegraph, but I think it would, being an official government department. It's worth a try!'

'We'll have to ride into Rio Blanco to send it,' Fargo pointed out. 'But the delay might well be worth it.'

'I can send the wire for you – you just write out what you wanta say, Dusty,' offered Price. She agreed instantly and went back into the house for paper and pencil then wrote out the message. It read:

To Gary Sloane, care Barnabas Indian agency
URGENT!
ENEMIES COMING TO KILL YOU.
ON WAY WITH HELP. TAKE PRECAUTIONS.
DUSTY.

'It'll be enough, I think – I hope!' she said, handing the paper to Price. Charge the message to the ranch account.'

Price nodded, folding the paper into his pocket. 'Satterlee better take it in. He's lighter'n me and a faster rider. Best you get goin', Dusty.' He gestured to the east where a very faint pale line was beginning to grow.

They mounted, Fargo settling the strange six-gun rig more comfortably on his thigh, and making sure the rifle was seated firmly in the saddle scabbard. Lockie Bruce was ready and waiting to move out, leading a packhorse.

There was little noise beyond the muted clop of hoofs as they cleared the yard and started out into the darkness beyond. . . .

Price turned towards the bunkhouse. Satterlee had taken the fast claybank, so he could likely make town in a couple of hours by cutting over Hashknife Ridge.

And that was the way Satterlee went. The winds of passage brought him fully awake and he arrived within the time predicted by Price.

The telegraph operator on duty had to be awakened, but, used to messages having to be sent or received at odd hours, was fully alert when Satterlee handed him Dusty's slip of paper.

His seamed face screwed up and he whistled softly through his lips even as his hand started tapping out recognition signals and the mysterious combinations of dots and dashes that only made sense to the initiated.

Yawning, Satterlee walked back to the claybank and led it to the livery. Damned if he was going to ride all the way back to Slash S that day. He'd sleep in the loft if old Tate would let him.

He was settling into his pile of hay by the time a man stepped into the telegraph shack just as the operator rattled the key on his sign-off. He spun in his chair, staring at the blond man who held a gun in his left hand.

'Hey! You can't come in here like—'

Bisby grabbed the man's right hand and despite the operator's struggles, spread it out on the edge of the counter. 'What the hell're you doin'? Lemme go! Lemme—'

'This hand makes your livin' for you, right?' Bisby was said, reversing his gun so that the butt was now poised above the man's spread fingers. 'Tell me what I want to know and you'll be all right. Gimme trouble and I'll turn your fingers into mashed bananas.' He rapped the heavy gun butt lightly against the operator's knuckles. The man yelped, struggled, trying to get out of the chair, but Bisby held him easily.

'Now, where you send that last message? Oh, forgot to tell you, I only ask my questions once, so consider the first one is due an answer – right – *now*!'

The man, streaming with sweat, fumbled at his spike file with his free hand and ripped Dusty's message off the top, waving it frantically at Bisby.

'Well, now, that's what I call co-operation. Now I want you to send a message to a couple of friends of mine, then you can tell me how to get to this Barnabas dump. OK?'

It was as rough a trail as Fargo had ever seen, and there had been some mighty rugged ones on the Pacific Coast of South America on the whaling run.

It wasn't so cold and bleak here, but the climb up the steep, rocky slopes took it out of their mounts and the loaded packhorses, requiring frequent stops.

'I was hoping we would make better time than this,'

Dusty said, face drawn with the effort, for they had had to dismount frequently and literally drag the horses across rocky barriers in parts.

Standing back after climbing to the top of a big, egg-shaped boulder, Fargo tilted his head and squinted into the sun. 'Looks like it eases some after about another twenty, thirty feet vertically. I can see a trail angling up, not very wide, but it rises gradually.'

Dusty lowered the canteen from her lips, wiped her chin and replaced the stopper. 'Well, I guess we'd better go up and see, but easy or hard, it's the only way . . . unless you want to ride all the way back down and take the longer trail around the range, instead of trying to go over it.'

'We'd lose too much time.'

Lockie Bruce said, 'Just been studying the crests yonder. I've been over this section once, long time back. The trail runs along the top. That should make it a lot easier.'

It took them the rest of the day to reach the trail that did indeed run along the ridge top. It was narrow but flat, with few sharp turns, and they made good time riding in Indian file. When they came out of some trees and found themselves on a large flat rock, Fargo sat straighter and whistled softly.

'Now that's the kind of view I missed when I was on the whaler.' He folded his hands on the saddlehorn and drank in the vista of rugged mountains, much of them clad in greenery; some with crests under a blanket of glaring white snow. 'I can savvy how Gary must like this kinda solitude.'

'Yes,' Dusty said, looking around. 'It's beautiful, but I'm afraid we don't have time to admire it. The sun will be down in another hour or so, but we should have time to get on to the next peak if we keep moving.'

'I'll ride on ahead and pick a campin' spot, if you like, Dusty,' offered Lockie, lighting a cigarette he had just made from Fargo's profferred tobacco sack and papers. He tossed the sack back and Fargo caught it, slipped it into his shirt pocket and drew on his own cigarette.

'Pick somewhere with a few rocks around it for protection,' Fargo advised. Lockie lifted a hand to his hatbrim in salute and rode off. Fargo got the packhorses moving and touched his heels to his mount's flanks. 'D'you have any idea how far it is to the agency? Or how far beyond it your uncle's trading post is?'

Dusty shook her head, face drawn. 'Not really, except that we have a long way to go yet.'

He decided not to mention that he thought he had seen a flash of bright blue among the greenery of trees and brush down in one of the draws earlier when they had been riding the crest. He had only glimpsed it once but it could have been a rider in a blue shirt. Then. . . .

'Why d'you keep turning and looking back – and down?' she asked suddenly, surprising him. 'Have you seen something?'

He made a quick decision. 'I think I might've seen a rider – just one. Which doesn't make sense. I'm certain sure a man like Bisby would hire some hardcases in a deal like this. Maybe he was just a scout

88

looking for our tracks.'

Her teeth tugged at her lower lip. 'I see now why you told Lockie to look for a campsite with rocks around it.'

'We'll mount guard.'

'Then I'll take my turn,' she told him flatly. 'And don't either you nor Lockie "forget" to wake me for it!'

She heeled her horse forward, her own packhorse following, and Fargo nudged his mount after her, silently admiring her spirit.

But he knew that with a man like Bisby it would always come down to guns. How would she stand up then?

How would any of them stand up against a cold-blooded killer who would more than likely have backup from men of his own kind?

Lockie Bruce had chosen a good place for a campsite should it need to be defended. There were rocks of various sizes and one afforded a view back down the slope the way they had travelled.

They ate cold grub and Lockie went to relieve himself behind a big boulder, afterwards, stepping up on to it and sitting there, letting his eyes get used to the darkness. A few minutes later he was sure he had seen a bright spot that could only mean a sloppily hidden camp-fire.

'It blotted out a couple times,' he added to his information back at the main camp. 'I guess there's a bunch of fellers down there movin' around.'

The girl's face was pale and taut with tension but

she said nothing as she drained her mug of water.

'Thought I saw a rider in a bright blue shirt this afternoon while you were looking for this camp site,' Fargo told Lockie. 'Reckon he was scouting for Bisby, and from what you saw from that rock, sounds like he's got backup.'

'Would make sense, I guess. I used to hunt these hills when my pa was alive: good turkey country. I know this part pretty well. How about I slip on down and see what I can find out?'

'No,' Fargo said immediately. 'Too damn risky, Lockie.'

'I can do it. My ma was a half-blood Sioux, my old man a Scotsman. Good combo, Craig! You got warrior blood on one side, and my pa was stubborn as a brush maverick. I've got the best of each part in me, right, Dusty?'

'That's true, Lockie, but Craig's right – it's too risky.'

'Nah, look, I can slip up and lie doggo, just close enough to make a head count, or hear what they're sayin'. I can do it, Dusty! Lemme try! George was good to me and I'd like to do more than just ride along with you and Fargo.'

They argued back and forth but in the end Dusty reluctantly agreed and before Fargo had finished his final argument, Lockie was tying hessian around his mount's hoofs. Then he checked his rifle, set his hat firmly and waved once before disappearing into the darkness.

Fargo strained to hear, but there was no sound of Lockie making his way back down the slope. So maybe there was a chance yet he could pull this off. . . .

'Should you go after him?' Dusty asked worriedly.

Fargo shook his head. 'I'd make more noise than he does – foul things up. He's keen and he seems to know this area pretty darn well. He'll be back – with info we can use.'

Her white teeth tugged at her lower lip as she nodded slowly.

'I hope so.'

Lockie Bruce was good at making his way silently down the slope. Just before he reached the bottom, he climbed on to a deadfall, checking the direction he had seen that spark earlier. *Yes!* There it was, a small splash of light between leaves or some saplings. He clambered down, levered a cartridge into the rifle's breech slowly and silently, then eased his way closer to what he now saw was a camp of several men.

Crouching, he used the rifle barrel to push aside a couple of small branches and counted six – no, seven – men. He recognized Al Bisby from Fargo's description: the man had his hat pushed back on his blond head as he licked a cigarette paper and put the slim cylinder in his mouth. He leaned towards the small camp-fire and lit it from a twig.

'Now I want you all to ride carefully, and *stay under cover*! We don't want to give ourselves away.'

'How come, Al?' asked a man with a full black beard. 'They's only three and we're eight. We can take 'em without missin' a draw on our smokes.'

Others murmured agreement, but Bisby shook his

head. 'I want 'em to lead us to this Sloane *hombre* – none of us know this country and. . . .'

Just about then Lockie Bruce went cold: that bearded man had said they were eight! And he had only counted seven around the camp-fire.

Where was the eighth man. . . ?

The cold ring of iron suddenly pressing into the back of his neck answered his question. A knee dropped on to his back, making his spine creak, as he gusted breath from his lungs.

'Don't be so unsociable, feller,' a rough voice said. 'Come on in an' join us!'

CHAPTER 9

BARNABAS

Lockie Bruce and his horse reached the campsite among the rocks some time after midnight. The moon was high, spilling silver light over the sleeping Fargo and Dusty Sloane.

But it was the welcoming whinny of their mounts and pack animals that woke them as Lockie's horse walked in and stopped near where they had spread their bedrolls.

Fargo rolled out of his blanket in a practised move taking his rifle with him, the lever working as he came up on one knee, the weapon ready to deal with any danger.

But not with what he saw.

The sweating horse stood near where Lockie had spread his blanket before he set off to reconnoitre Bisby's camp. It shook its head and whinnied quietly again. Bruce leaned precariously to the left in the saddle.

He was roped in place, slumped forward from the waist now. Fargo, holding the rifle, stepped up swiftly and grabbed the mount's bridle. It snorted and again the movement caused Lockie to sway, head lolling. Dusty gasped and Fargo lowered the rifle hammer, set the weapon against a rock as he stepped around the horse's head and stood by the left stirrup.

'Lockie?' he said quietly, but he was close enough now to see there would be no reply.

The young cowboy's shirt was slashed in several places, splashed with much blood, and he was hatless, so that the many red streaks and cuts and burns disfiguring his face showed black in the wan moonlight. Dusty put a hand to her mouth. 'Oh, my God! What – what've they done to him?'

'Gimme a hand to get him down,' Fargo said curtly. Between them they cut the ropes and Fargo took Lockie's weight and eased him to the spread blanket.

'Oh, dear Lord, he's *dead*! And there's – there's something on the front of his shirt.'

Fargo saw it then: a piece of paper, splashed with blood, pinned to Bruce's shirt with a sharpened twig. There were words written on it, mostly illegible because of the blood that had soaked the paper.

'Can't make 'em out. . . . They turned him loose on his mount, figuring it'd make its way back to our camp.' He looked keenly around shadowed, light-splashed rocks and trees. 'They could've followed, but I've a feeling that note'll tell us what they expect of us next.'

She gasped as he stepped behind a big rock and

scraped a vesta across the rough surface. 'What're you doing? We make a damn fine target right now if they're out there!'

'Even if they are, and I doubt it, I think they're waiting for us to make some kind of move and won't bother us till we do, maybe not even then.' He could see she didn't understand but he was in no mood to explain his hunch right now. 'If they followed Lockie up here, they can't see us behind this rock. You stay in the shadows while I see what the note says.'

Dusty had her rifle and hunkered down swiftly in the deep shadow between two rocks, looking around anxiously.

'Can you read it?' He held the paper so the match flame showed the words and Dusty could just make them out.

' "C U there – if you hurry!" Is that right?' He nodded and she added, puzzled, 'But what. . . ? Where're they talking about?'

'Gary's place, I reckon.' He heard her draw in a sharp breath. 'They've obviously tortured Lockie and he must've told them where the trading post is.'

'He couldn't, because he doesn't – didn't – know!' Dusty said sharply. 'Gary doesn't advertise his trading post! It's mostly for Indians. I don't even know for sure where it is, just a general notion, but I'm hoping that the agency has sent someone to warn him after they got my wire, and he'll go back to the agency with them for safety.'

'Well, mebbe Bisby meant he'll see us at the Indian agency.'

There was a brief hesitation before she said, 'Most anyone could tell them where that is. They wouldn't need to do what they did to Lockie!'

He could hear the tremor in her voice as the shock of it all started to hit home. 'Then they must mean Gary's.'

'I just told you! Lockie didn't know where Gary's trading post is!'

Fargo was silent as Dusty choked back a sob. He grabbed his blanket and covered up the bloody body. 'There's another angle,' he said quietly. 'Mebbe Lockie didn't tell them anything at all.'

She dabbed at her eyes jerkily with a small kerchief. 'He *couldn't* tell them anything because he didn't know where Gary lives!'

'So this is likely Al Bisby tryin' to be smart. He'd reckon *you* know where the trading post is, and he's hoping the note will panic us into running straight to Gary's: all they have to do is follow.'

'Of course: they didn't know Lockie *couldn't* tell them anything except about a very general area. But the note was designed to make us think he had, and they're already on their way to Gary's – that's why the note says, "If you hurry". Is that what you mean?'

Fargo nodded. 'They're out there somewhere, watching, waiting for *us* to lead them to the trading post. And we would've, if the note'd worked the way they expected.'

She was looking around now, head jerking quickly this way and that, fingers white where they clutched her rifle. 'You think they're watching? Now?'

'If I'm right about the note they likely are. They're waiting for us to make the next move.'

'Well – what are we going to do?'

'Pack up and light a shuck.'

'And where do we lead them?'

'Only one place we can lead them – the Barnabas agency. The people there obviously know where Gary lives. You said the agency was kinda "off-beat". What did you mean?'

'I'm not quite sure, just that they're trying some sort of new approach to how we look after the Indian tribes. I don't know any details but—'

'Never mind. We've got to get going – now.'

He heard her swallow nervously.

'We've got to make it look good, move fast with lots of fumbling. Make 'em think we really are in a big panic.'

'I won't have to fake my panic! What about Lockie?'

'We'll have to take him with us. No time now to give him a decent burial. I'll tie him across his horse. Someone at Barnabas will see to him, won't they?'

She just nodded and started throwing her things together. She was right: she didn't have to fake the panic.

It was dangerous riding those hills in the dark, and, moreover, they were climbing all the time. Some parts the rise was gradual and relatively easy, but other places they had to dismount and lead their horses until they reached an area where they could once again climb into the saddle.

The horses were feeling the strain. Some of it would be caused by their natural reluctance to move over such country in the darkness, but mostly it would be their inbuilt instincts, telling them here was danger with a capital 'D'.

They had left Lockie's packhorse behind at the campsite, just heaving off the pack-saddle and letting the contents scatter and lay there: it would add to the 'state of panic' that they were trying to convey to Al Bisby and 'friends'. Fargo was sure Bisby would have called in help. He'd already made one serious mistake in killing the wrong Sloane, and he wouldn't risk another. He would be a bit leery about Gary Sloane, too. A man couldn't lead the kind of life Gary did without being mighty tough and resourceful.

Bisby's sort didn't ride into those kinds of situations without taking precautions. . . .

He had said nothing of this to Dusty, allowing her to lead the way, only going forward to help her in really rough places. She might suspect something along the lines he had been thinking, but he kept talk to a minimum and dropped back as soon as his assistance was no longer required. He watched as she moved around a lot when in the saddle, looking behind and down.

Fargo preferred to keep his checking to the higher country. If he was following someone through these hills he would try to get higher or at least on the same level. He wouldn't follow from *below*: it was risking discovery, with the quarry viewing from above. But then, the ridges seemed more broken here than earlier so it would be hard to stay in position – and the horses would be sure to scatter stones that could roll down and alert any riders at a lower level.

In other words, it was all a matter of tossing a mental coin, and hoping it came down 'heads' – *and* that 'heads' was the side that counted.

His thoughts had kept him so busy that he almost rode into an eroded draw, fighting his mount as its hammering hoofs broke away the edges. It snorted in protest, stomped and backed up, twisting around to try and bite his leg.

'What on earth happened?' asked the girl in a husky voice, having reined down ahead and slightly above him.

'My fault – didn't see the draw in time. We're OK.'

'You've made enough noise to give anyone following a perfect direction!'

He detected the nervousness in her voice and refrained from snapping a reply. 'They know exactly where we are, Dusty. But I'll be more careful.'

'You should be!'

He smiled thinly: she was worried, likely plain scared, so he didn't mind her taking out her nervous tension on him.

'How close are we to the sgency?' he asked quietly.

'Follow me and find out! And just watch where you're going.'

'Yes, ma'am!'

He deliberately delayed by a clump of boulders on the near side of a crest, making out he was checking for a stone under his mount's right forefoot. His vision was pretty well used to the dark now and he hunkered down, the horse's foot across his bent knee, but while his fingers checked for stones, his eyes swept over the dark slopes.

There was movement of some kind behind and a little above, which meant Bisby's riders were following the crests – risky, but it would give them a better view of the slopes. . . .

He couldn't tell how many riders there were but he figured at least six, likely more.

When he mounted he slid his rifle from the scabbard and worked the lever as quietly as possible, easing down the hammer before he rammed the Winchester back into leather. *He wasn't the kind to risk riding with a loaded gun under a cocked hammer – not in this kind of terrain – if ever.*

Next instant, Dusty was reining up beside him.

'What did you see?' she hissed her face showed pale, barely a foot from his own.

He gestured vaguely upslope. 'Just playing it safe.'

'Don't treat me like this, Fargo! Yes, I'm scared, but I'll – I'll fight right alongside you when it's necessary. I'm a good shot.'

'Ever shot a man?'

A hesitation, then a quiet 'No', followed by a shaking of the head.

'*Could* you shoot one?'

A longer hesitation this time. 'I – I'm not sure.'

That was the answer he wanted: she'd do it, all right. Determination would help her squeeze the trigger and direct the bullet. If she'd replied with an emphatic

'Yes!' he would've been worried, because then she would have been merely saying it because her courage had been questioned.

But Dusty Sloane had more sense than to raise her hackles over such an important subject.

At the same time, of course, she hoped like hell the occasion would never arise. . . .

When they finally reached the dark agency it was close to sunup. The building was several hundred yards up slope from the Reservation proper: they could smell the smoke of breakfast fires and the odour of cooking food.

After rousing the agent, Cameron Breck, a man in his thirties with a bushy moustache Fargo figured he wore to make himself look more mature, they were told news they didn't want to hear.

'No, Gary's not here, Dusty,' Breck answered her question. 'I didn't send a man out to his place.'

Dusty's eyes blazed. 'For heavens' sake, why not? I requested it in the wire! It's essential that Gary be warned his life is in danger!'

Breck shook his head slowly, holding up one hand as he started to rummamge among some papers on his battered desk top. 'I got your wire and was making arrangements for a man to ride post-haste to Gary's trading post, when your second wire came in.'

'What second wire?' Dusty asked, blinking.

'Here it is.' Breck handed her a slip of paper and Fargo saw her hands were shaking as she took it and read:

Sorry. Mistaken. No danger for Gary. Ignore first message. Will explain when I arrive.
Dusty.

She looked up sharply at Fargo, face white. 'I never sent this!'

'It would've been Bisby.' Fargo told her. 'So Mr Breck here wouldn't bother sending anyone to warn Gary.'

'Then Gary's still unaware he's in danger!' She snapped her head around to look at the frowning agent. 'We'll need a guide, Mr Breck. Can you furnish one?'

'Of course, but I don't understand what's going on.'

'It's too complicated to explain right now. We have to get to Gary! His life's in danger!'

'Slow down, Dusty,' Fargo said quietly and she frowned. 'This is Bisby bein' smart again. He must've made the telegraph operator in Rio Blanco send this right after your message. He couldn't've known about Lockie at the time but this was planned to do exactly what that note he pinned to Lockie's shirt was intended to: cause us to panic and run straight to Gary – leading Bisby right there.'

She looked quickly out the window, which was showing clearly now with the imminent sunrise. 'But he's followed us here!'

'Only because we didn't know the way to Gary's.' Fargo lifted his rifle. 'Might be a good idea you turn out that lamp, Mr Breck. Makes a good target.'

As he spoke, the lamp on the desk exploded, spraying a fan of hot oil. An instant afterwards a bullet smashed through the window. Fortunately, the oil did not ignite.

But the first bullet was quickly followed by a fusilade of others, too many and too fast to count. They shattered the rest of the window, rattled the door in its frame and splintered the desk itself, sending papers flying like leaves in a wind. Splinters hummed dangerously at face level as Fargo dragged Dusty down beside him. Breck was already crouched by his desk.

Fargo brought up his rifle and triggered three swift shots through the gaping window, then thrust the weapon into the girl's hands as he drew the six-gun she had provided him with earlier.

'Now's the time when you have to make that decision we were talking about earlier.'

She looked puzzled for a moment and then blood drained from her face: she knew what he meant.

Now was when she would find out if she *could* kill a man.

CHAPTER 10

RESTORATION TRAIL

Cameron Breck suddenly lunged up from beside the desk and snatched a rifle down from a set of wooden pegs on the wall. He made a half-gasp, half-curse as he dropped the rifle and flopped to the floor, nursing a bullet-creased wrist.

'Bad?' asked Fargo, now crouched to one side and below the shattered window.

Breck gritted, 'I'll manage!' Craig Fargo rose and triggered two swift shots, dropping back and skidding the smoking Colt across to the Indian agent.

'You might be able to handle that better than the rifle – swap.'

'It's yours.'

The rifle spun across the floor and as he snatched it up, Fargo recognized it as a brass-actioned Henry: so there should be fourteen shots in the magazine, and maybe one in the breech. *Just what he needed!* The legendary rifle you 'load on Sunday and shoot all week'!

'There's at least half a dozen of 'em out there,' he said, levering and lifting up to snap three fast shots at the shadows that were shooting back. Splinters flew from a corral rail and he thought one man toppled sideways as he ducked back, sending at least four bullets to tear up the window frame. Dusty was at a second window and Breck told her to smash it. She did so with the rifle barrel, and started firing.

Breck himself was shooting from a corner of the window where Fargo crouched. They saw men scattering, triggered without seeing the results of their shooting.

Then Al Bisby's voice cut through the echoes of gunfire.

'Fargo! I know you're a horse lover. We got us a couple corrals full of 'em out here. We're gonna start gutshootin' 'em till you come out with your hands up! That sound OK?'

Fargo's lips compressed and he fired his shot in the direction of the voice: that ought to be answer enough. The girl looked at him, her face wild.

'You can't let him kill all those horses!'

'Can't let him kill us, either.'

They both looked at Breck who, surprisingly, smiled. 'Just wait a minute!'

'The hell for?' Fargo snapped as rifles cracked outside and horses whinnied frantically.

'That!' answered Breck with satisfaction.

Neither Dusty nor Fargo believed what they were hearing at first: wild Indian war-whoops and the thunder of unshod hoofs.

Gunshots rattled; rifles and six-guns and at least one shotgun. Men were shouting but their words were drowned out by the cries of the dozen or so Indians who thundered in from the Reservation on the slope below the agency administration buildings and Breck's living quarters.

Obviously they had been drawn by the gunfire. Through the shattered windows they watched as Bisby's men ran for their mounts. Two were shot down and only one got to his feet, favouring one leg as he limped after the main group. No one stopped to help him; his companions were mounted or half-mounted, one man simply hanging across his saddle as they set the horses running – upslope, downslope, across the slope – any direction that would take them out of range of the Indian bucks. The wounded man finally caught a horse and clambered awkwardly on board.

Breck ran to the door, triggered his last two shots and some of the racing Indians looked back. He made swift 'come-back' gestures. They slowed and, reluctantly, Fargo thought, sat their panting ponies, before wheeling towards the agency building. It was now pock-marked with bullets and light-coloured streaks showed where long splinters had been sheared from the logs.

'Didn't know Reservation Indians were allowed firearms,' Fargo commented.

'You complaining?' Breck asked, unsmiling and

Fargo shook his head. 'This is an experimental agency and Reservation, Fargo. There are enlightened people in government who realize the main cause of differences between us and the Indians is that we took away their way of life. Sure, we fed them, on government rations, a diet worked out by well-meaning people in Washington, but they longed to – *needed* to hunt and trap and gather wild foods as has been their way of life long before white men ever set foot on this continent.'

Fargo nodded and Dusty, too, but she was showing more interest in what Breck was saying than Fargo was.

'I'm fairly new here – in fact, I've only met Dusty once before – but I have the backing of a powerful group and we hope to make this Reservaton a model for future ones, if our experiment is successful.'

'So far, I'm glad it's working out,' Fargo admitted. 'Not saying the idea's bad or good but it's kinda radical, isn't it?'

'Yes. The politician behind it, Martin Winfield, is a man of vision. In fact, we're being honoured with a visit from him in the not too distant future. He's running on this pro-Indian "ticket" as they call it for his election platform. There's been a lot of opposition, of course, but less than expected, so we're confident it will get him into the White House to form a new Pro-Indian Party.'

'Be good to see, but wouldn't count on it,' Fargo opined, reloading the six-gun and rifles.

'You did mention something to that effect the one time we met, Mr Breck,' Dusty said. 'But I didn't realize how far along the experiment had come.'

'Yes. The Easterners seem to think we're having some success – enough, anyway, that they can use for their election campaign, I suppose.'

He smiled and Dusty smiled back. 'Well, I guess you don't mind that. . . .'

Her voice trailed off as a bunch of horses came up to the front of the building. Fargo paused in his reloading and stared at a big Indian with braided hair, in checked shirt and buckskin trousers who appeared in the doorway. He raked the trio with jet black eyes.

'All right, Mr Breck?' he asked in accented but good American English.

'Thanks to your timely arrival, Herb.' Breck gestured to him and spoke to Dusty and Fargo. 'This is Dusty Sloane and Craig Fargo. Meet Herbert Lightfoot, our chief officer of the Reservation, though we delete the "officer" part and simply call him Chief Lightfoot.'

The Indian came in with outstretched hand and shook briefly with Fargo after bowing his head slightly towards Dusty.

'Howdy, Chief,' Fargo said, gripping and feeling the strength in those dark fingers. 'Good timing.'

'Mr Breck cares for our people. It is only right we care for him – when he needs it.' He smiled, adding, 'And it felt good to ride bareback again and use the old war cries – very good.'

'Lightfoot is Santee Sioux, went to a mission school in Denver,' Breck explained. 'Speaks better English than I do.'

'Chief Lightfoot,' Dusty said, looking anxious, 'Can

you guide us to the Restoration trading post? Gary is my uncle and his life is in danger. That first urgent wire I sent was no mistake, but was cancelled by the man who just led the attack on this agency.'

'He is the one who intends to kill Gary?' the big Sioux asked, and as Dusty nodded, said, 'a pity we didn't know or we'd have run him and his men down. I will guide you to Gary's place.'

'Chief, Al Bisby, that man who wanted to shoot the horses, won't give up just because you and your warriors drove him away from here. He'll be somewhere back there, watching. And he'll follow.'

Lightfoot nodded. 'Of course, but perhaps he will be watching us so closely, he does not see my men who will be watching him.'

Fargo grinned. 'You've learned more than how to speak English I see.'

Lightfoot shook his head. 'No, no need to learn some things – they come from my people, and all Sioux know them. We will leave soon. Very soon.'

There was no sign of Al Bisby and the remainder of his men.

One man had been killed during the attack on the agency, and there was a lot of blood that led to where a horse had been standing in another spot, which indicated that someone had been wounded pretty seriously.

Fargo had estimated – he couldn't be sure in the half-light and the unceasing movement of the attackers – that Bisby had had at least six to eight men with him. If this number was correct, it meant there were still six left to deal with, including Bisby. Then again, possibly only five, depending on how badly the wounded man was hit.

Lightfoot led the way, but he turned downslope, angling back the way Dusty and Fargo had come. She rode up alongside Fargo, frowning, and shrugged her shoulders as if to ask, 'What's he doing?'.

Fargo spurred his mount after the Indian and came up alongside as the man stopped on a ledge, once again studying the slope *below*.

'Figured the trading post was on the crest, Chief.'

Lightfoot nodded without looking at Fargo. 'We'll get there.'

'How, if we're going down, when we should be going up?'

The Indian looked squarely at Fargo now. 'I know a quicker way.'

'Well, I don't see it, Chief, but you're in charge.'

Lightfoot pointed below. 'We go into those trees. They're thick enough to hide our movements from above. You and Dusty come with me and we'll lose Bisby – if he's still following.'

Fargo hesitated briefly before saying, 'Chief, you know this country better than me – I'll trust you on Breck's say-so – but don't underestimate Al Bisby. He's a hired killer and according to what he said in Rio Blanco, he has protection from someone high up in government, I guess, I'm not sure. What I'm saying, is he's not going to give up. You can tie our trail in knots and he'll unravel 'em somehow and be there when we ride in to Restoration.'

Lightfoot nodded soberly. 'I have met many men like that, that's why I have taken precautions.'

Fargo looked around expressively. 'You hide 'em well.'

Herb Lightfoot laughed briefly. 'You're a typical white man, Fargo – don't savvy the red man's way of thinking.'

Fargo smiled crookedly. 'You're right there, *amigo*. But like I said, you're in charge.'

When he dropped back beside Dusty, who was as puzzled as he was, he just shrugged. 'He knows what he's doing – he says.'

She was anxious, not really doubting the Indian's ability, but not knowing his plan was stringing out her nerves. . . .

So they rode on into the trees and after travelling a meandering route for a mile, Lightfoot held up a hand and they paused on a ledge above a narrow stream. It cascaded in a minature waterfall in the direction Fargo figured they ought to go – if much lower down than he would have thought – and Lightfoot made a listening movement with his head.

The girl looked briefly at Fargo, started to speak, then suddenly drew down a deep breath.

'*Shooting*! I – I'm sure I heard gunfire.' She looked up to the slopes above and the Indian nodded.

'Your friend Bisby was so busy trailing us and, like you, trying to figure out why we go downslope instead of up, that he didn't notice my men coming up behind.'

111

Fargo straightened in the saddle, hearing the scattered gunfire now. 'He's not the only one! Where the hell are they?'

'Back there, lost in the shadows, until they are ready to show themselves.'

Fargo grinned. 'You sure you didn't *teach* at that Denver school, instead of bein' a student?'

'Told you once – Indians have their own ways of doing things. If you're happy with what I have done, we'll head upwards now.'

'What about Bisby?' Dusty asked.

'He'll be busy for a while yet. By the time he can break away from my men, if they allow it, it'll be dark again and he won't find any trail. That's if he's still alive.'

Dusty jerked her head up. 'Your men are trying to . . . kill him?'

'He plans to kill you when you have led him to Gary's, doesn't he?' Dusty's teeth tugged at her lower lip as she nodded slowly. Lightfoot grinned again. 'You see? I am still more red than white.'

'A man's outside colour don't make no nevermind,' Fargo said quietly.

Lightfoot held his gaze soberly for a long minute before nodding. 'We ride.'

The sounds of shooting died away before they had ridden upslope and through a draw that led to yet another slope. After half an hour's hard climbing they reached a trail along the crest – a trail only Lightfoot could find – and the going was much easier.

They all did their share of watching the country

behind but none of them claimed to have seen anyone following.

'Does that mean your men have killed Bisby and his men?' Dusty asked.

'Probably not – just messed up his head a little.' Fargo said. 'Bisby'd be no loss.'

'No, but too many dead white men this close to a Reservation would bring in the army to investigate, and there are those who would twist things to make the Indian the villain of the piece. You'll find the pro-Indian supporters are mostly in the cities, Fargo – not many out here.'

Craig Fargo merely nodded, but he thought that Herb Lightfoot was a much smarter man than he had allowed. . . .

It was getting on towards sundown – still early after-noon, really, but the shadows thrown by the hills gave the impression of night closing in – when the Indian reined in on a rise and pointed ahead. If it hadn't been for the thin column of smoke – from a chimney, probably – climbing lazily into the cool mountain air, they would have missed seeing the corner of a shingle roof just showing through the trees.

'Restoration trading post,' Lightfoot said. 'By the time we get there, it should be about supper time. I hope Gary's killed a deer recently – I have a craving for some nice tender venison.'

He spurred forward and the weary Dusty and Fargo followed, with the packhorses trailing behind.

But Fargo paused on the highest part of the slope, looking back. He didn't see any pursuers, but he knew

113

a man like Bisby wouldn't give up easily.
They would need to stay on their toes.

CHAPTER 11

THE RAID

The middle-aged man standing by the door of the trading post had to be Gary Sloane, Fargo reckoned. He was dressed in buckskins and wearing a round fur hat decorated with a band made out of bears' claws sewn close together.

A couple of inches taller than Dusty, he was slim with it. His beard and moustache were short, clean, and streaked liberally with steel grey. What skin showed was leathery and rifle-butt dark, pale green eyes enhancing this effect. Fargo glimpsed yellow teeth with a few gaps. He was holding a Sharps Big Fifty, a rifle familiar to Craig Fargo from his long-ago days as a buffalo hunter-in-the-making.

Gary nodded briefly to Lightfoot and his lips spread slightly as he saw Dusty. He flicked his gaze to Fargo and frowned, shoulders stiffening. Fargo was somewhat startled to see the man's knuckles whiten where his hand held the Big fifty.

'By all that's Holy! Just for a moment I thought you were Morgan Fargo! You'd have to be his kid, right?'

His voice belonged to the wilderness: the quiet, yet far-reaching sound of a man who was part of Nature, had no need to raise his voice; likely spoke to no one but animals – and himself – Fargo figured.

'I'm Craig Fargo – Pa's dead. Man named Tyson killed him.'

Gary Sloane stiffened again and he lifted the rifle across his chest now. 'Now that's a name I haven't heard in a long, long time. So Tyson's still alive.'

Fargo shook his head. 'I killed him – about eight years ago now.'

Gary stared. 'You must've been young.'

'Fifteen – and not fast enough to save Pa.'

Sloane blew out his cheeks. 'Folks, you better come inside. I reckon you've got plenty more to tell.' He flicked his gaze from Dusty, to Lightfoot, to Fargo. 'I'm just roastin' a haunch of venison. Ah! See that gets your interest, Lightfoot.'

'That's not thunder rumbling in the hills you hear – it's my belly!'

Gary almost smiled. 'Well, let's go fill it up, there's plenty to go round. Then we can talk.'

Gary Sloane listened silently to Fargo's story about the attack on the mountain cabin.

'Sounds like mebbe Tyson was behind it. He was always a mean cuss, toady to another mean one – Captain Wyndham.'

'Pa never had a chance to say much, but he was

116

mighty anxious that I track down you and the others.'

'Took you eight years?' There was censure in Gary's voice until he heard how Craig had been shanghai'd into a whaler. 'And soon as you got back you started on it again?'

Fargo shrugged. 'I hadn't found any of you except those buffalo runners, and they were murdered by Al Bisby.'

'Why did you think it was necessary to keep lookin' after all that time?'

'Because it was Pa's last wish. He really wanted me to find you men and warn you about what had happened . . . and he said you'd "take care" of me. Someone he trusted to look out for me.'

Gary nodded. 'Yeah, well, you don't seem as if you need much "takin' care of", but we all made the vow to Morgan that if anythin' happened to him, *whenever*, we'd look out for you. You'd've only been a shaver at that time. Your ma was still alive, but ailin'.'

'But why did he ask you men?' It was something that had puzzled Craig for years and he saw Dusty nod gently: she had wondered, too.

Gary's explanation was both succinct and simple: 'Your pa saved all our lives, Craig, includin' that snake Tyson's. Takin' care of you was our way of payin' him back.'

Suddenly standing, Lightfoot reached to the central wooden platter and took a thick hunk of venison. 'I would like to hear more but I think someone should be outside,' he said quietly, 'on guard.' He went out the door, taking his rifle with him, chewing on the meat. Gary's gaze followed him.

'Bisby could still be out there,' Craig warned.

Gary pursed his lips, studying Fargo carefully. 'We were all together during the war, under Captain Mark Wyndham. Tyson was his lieutenant. Your pa was a sergeant in our specialist artillery squad. Ever heard of mortar bombing?'

Dusty hadn't but Fargo knew. 'Lobbing fifty-pound explosive shells on to a target you don't even have to see?'

'Yeah, shoot over a mountain, a row of houses, or a ridge and drop 'em on the target on the other side – and not be seen doing it. Your pa and me were the spotters, directing the fire.' He smiled, remembering. 'The Yankees had mortars, too, of course, but "Wyndham's Bombers" as we were known officially, were the best.'

It was obvious Gary's thoughts had gone back in time as he nodded, almost absently. 'Yeah, we were the experts. So when a big Yankee target just had to be destroyed, we were the ones sent downriver by steamboat as far as it could go. Then we built rafts, loaded our mortars and shells on and poled the rest of the way. We were after a Yankee cavalry outfit on the plains beyond a mountain range; we'd got word they were gathering for a big attack on our men to the north. Our supply lines were already cut; a raid like they were planning would've crippled us.'

Gary's voice seemed very distant now: his mind had taken him back to those last desperate, bloody days of the war, living once again that do-or-die raid. . . .

The landing place was in a hooked curve of the river – later named 'Hellfire Bend' – and they arrived just after sundown. Captain Wyndham was a professional soldier but not a very impressive looking man – medium height, slightly over-weight – but his military record told of remarkable feats of bravery, some said stupidity. Even in the days before the war, he had distinguished himself as an Indian fighter, was captured once and horribly tortured: some said it distorted his mind, left him with a pathological hatred for all Indians. Plus, way back before that, something had happened to his family. He never spoke about it in detail, only that renegade Apaches had wiped out all of his kinfolk. Then, later, his own days of torture at Apache hands had only served to reinforce this bitter hostility.

He was an arrogant, tough fighter and those men under him might have respected the rank, but never the man. He was tyrannical and abused his rank and any man in his command who had any sense trod mighty carefully. . . .

He had been expressly chosen for this raid because it was in the Indian country he had scouted and fought over in pre-war days. Wyndham jumped at the chance, keen to demonstrate that his mortar squad was truly the *best*. . . .

The landing place also became their attack position. There were ten men in the raiding party: two sets of four would service the two cast-brass mortars. The remaining two would act as spotters, climbing the steep mountain that began only yards from the landing place and from where they could signal the strike of the mortar shells. A good spotter could place the shells exactly on target within minutes of opening fire. Gary Sloane and Sergeant Morgan Fargo were the best spotters Wyndham could lay his hands on.

Captain Wyndham and Lieutenant Tyson drove the mortar teams relentlessly in their preparations. The men had been told by Colonel Clarke at Fort Shipton, their base, that it was a vital mission, but dangerous because they would have to make their own way back after the raid – if it was successful. If it wasn't, there was only a long stretch in a Yankee prison camp and, eventually, a firing squad awaiting them.

'But this *will* be a success, men!' Wyndham said just before he sent Gary Sloane and Morgan Fargo up the mountain. 'It *has* to be, so the South can gain a breathing space. The goddamn Yankees have crippled our production potential, cut our supply lines, and all we can do now is go down fighting! So, let's make this raid one that'll deserve its place in the history books!'

Tyson did his best to whip up some enthusiasm but there was no more than a scattered murmuring of assent.

A mite sourly, Wyndham continued: 'I can tell you now that we are using a new style of powder. Black powder tends to clog, as you know, with even a little moisture, but munitions have devised something to encase the grains, some kind of glaze, so that they slide much easier. Extra oxygen is trapped inside the casing so the powder burns quicker and it adds a mite more power to the explosion.'

The captain was now rocking back and forth on his heels and toes, and when he stopped, his left boot lifted slightly and the instep rubbed up and down against the muscle of his right leg beneath his dusty trousers. The squad knew from past experience that this was a characteristic sign that he was mighty edgy. He cleared his throat and snapped his orders, sending the spotters hurrying up the mountain, cussing the rest to greater speed. Tyson repeated Wyndham's commands like an echo . . . and with no more success.

The heavy mortars were dragged off the rafts on improvised sapling skids, the men straining, sweating liberally. The rafts were pushed into the shallows, ready for the getaway later. More saplings and packed earth were used to level the mortars' carriages to form stable firing bases. Wyndham directed their position with his compass and a map, making some quick calculations.

'We have to propel our shells a good fifteen hundred feet over this damn mountain, so we'll try a pound and a half of powder for a start,' he ordered the gunners. The appropriate size of copper scoops was selected in the growing light, dipped into the burlap-wrapped cask of black powder and placed in linen cartridge bags. These were placed firmly into the gaping maws of the mortars.

'What length of fuse are you using on the shells?' the captain snapped.

'Five-inch for ground detonation, Captain,' replied

Gunner Welch. 'About four and a quarter if you want an air explosion.'

'Try one of each. Lieutenant, cut the four and a quarter – no, make that four inches, I think; Welch can try just under five inches. The spotters will tell us which produces the best results.'

Wyndham took his field glasses and swept the lenses around the high slopes. Sloane was almost in position and Fargo was already in place, setting out his signal cloths: red meant the shot had landed too far over the target; white, too short, green, dead on.

The light was increasing fast now. The gunners were making last minute adjustments as their teams used the jackbars to bring the rear of the mortars up higher while some rocks were placed beneath for extra steadiness. Fargo signalled he was ready and a minute later, Gary Sloane did the same.

The captain used his left hand to direct the jackbar teams in lining up the mortars for the calculated direction of fire. The slow fuses were burning in the hands of the gunners; the cloth cartridges under the touchholes had already been pierced. Wyndham's hand sliced through the air like a falling axe, and the glowing tips of the slow-burning matches were thrust into the touch-holes on the mortars. The men clapped their hands over their ears as the stubby guns bellowed their thunder, recoil making them jump on their carriages. The shells rocketed up and over the mountain, tiny cigarette-sized dots of red trailing tendrils of smoke as their fuses burned. Even the bulk of the mountain couldn't deaden the sound of the explosions in the cavalry camp beyond. The shell fused to detonate in the air made the first blast, followed, seconds later, by the other ploughing into the ground among the rows of pitched tents where men were beginning to stir. Flame and earth gushed skyward, with twisted bodies among the debris and the blazing canvas of the demolished tents. The shell that had detonated in the air did so harmlessly over the cook shack. Wyndham and the gun teams couldn't see this: only the spotters were witness and made appropriate signals – Sloane's was green, Fargo's white.

While the chaos spread in the bombed camp, dozens of terrified horses in nearby corrals started to shrill and buck and kick and smash at the rails. Wyndham shouted orders. The mortars were re-aligned, powder charges cut by a few spoonsful; jsckbars were stabbed and lifted and pried under the mortar stands. The two gunners quickly rammed their loads of death home. . . .

'Fire! Fire! Fire!' screamed the captain, running from one mortar to the other, checking trajectories.

The sweating gunners and straining bar-men jumped back as the mortars again roared their lethal chorus and hurled their murderous messengers over the ranger. . . .

The signals came back; minor adjustments were made. The mortars thundered again – and again – and again – until there came a tremendous explosion that made the entire mountain tremble. Wyndham blinked as roiling smoke in thick, dark columns twisted up into the morning air, carrying with it broken trees and bodies of men and horses.

'What the devil. . . ?' Wyndham shouted, ears ringing.

Morgan Fargo stood up and cupped his hands around his mouth. His voice carried clearly as the echoes of the huge explosion died slowly:

'We hit the powder magazine, Capt'n! God almighty, there's one helluva crater!'

He and Sloane skidded and slid and stumbled their way back to the firing positions, panting, eyes wide with the shock of what they had witnessed.

'Total destruction, Capt'n,' Gary gasped. 'God, dead men and horses strewn all over the countryside!' He paused, spat as if to rid his mouth of some foul taste. 'I feel kinda sick. They didn't know where the attack was comin' from – just panicked, ran round like a bunch of chickens with their heads cut off!' He suddenly turned aside, retching. Lieutenant Tyson curled a sneering lip.

Wyndham flicked his gaze to the pale Fargo. 'Then we've done our job well, and we've still plenty of ammunition left over! It won't be wasted, I assure you!'

'Captain, there's nothin', *nothin'* left over that mountain worth wastin' a shell on,' Fargo assured him.

'I need to see for myself for my report, Sergeant. Have the men load the mortars back on to the rafts, while I climb up and look. Lieutenant, come with me.'

The men exchanged shocked glances. 'Cap'n,' said Fargo, 'I thought we was to dump the mortars in the river, then raft our way out downstream?'

'Then you thought wrong! I see no point in

"dumping" perfectly good weapons when there is still a use for them. I am charged with testing this new-fangled powder and I have in mind another target where we can confirm our first impressions. You have my orders!' Wyndham's face was wild, congested, a heavy pulse throbbing in his neck. His fingers were white where he wrung them in his shaking hands. 'Make sure the spare ammunition and powder can't get wet.' He smiled in a disturbing way they had never seen before. 'We'll have good cause to use it on our way home.' Then he surprised them by adding, 'And I should point out that, under military law, you are all automatically hereby sworn to secrecy – under pain of death never to speak about this mission, nor the one to follow!'

As they watched him commence the climb up the mountain with Tyson tagging along, Sloane said, 'Christ! We stop to hit another damn camp and the Yankees'll catch up!'

'The man's gripped by blood lust,' said Fargo quietly. 'First time I've seen it happen, but I've heard talk. They say he goes plumb loco when it's got him in its grip.'

Gary Sloane added in a hushed voice, 'Personally, I think he is a mite loco. Result of that Injun torture I guess, but *hell*!' He punched one hand into the other in frustration.

The others allowed they'd heard some wild stories about Wyndham's behaviour, too. But they got to work dragging the rafts closer inshore, all strangely quiet now. They struggled and strained to get the heavy mortars on board, one on each raft. It was mighty hard work, the men standing armpit-deep in the cold water.

When Wyndham returned, flushed, breathless and sweating, his eyes were alight with a strange excitement. Gary couldn't decide whether it was because of what he'd seen on the other side of the mountain, or anticipation of what was yet to come. . . .

Lieutenant Tyson ordered three men over the mountain to the devastated camp beyond: *to collect any uniforms, no matter how bloody or ragged, also any weapons lying about.* . . .

'And make damn sure they're marked clearly with the Yankee "US",' the captain broke in. . . .

In Gary Sloane's dimly lit cabin, the mountain man ran his gaze over his captive audience.

'Downstream there was another target, but he wouldn't say what: except that it was important it be destroyed. Then he "officially" swore all of us to secrecy again before we prepared for the attack. He said he'd do his own spotting this time, with his toady, Tyson, as back up. Obviously he didn't want anyone to know what the target was, but he was the superior officer and we had to follow his orders.'

'You must've had some idea of the target,' Dusty said.

Gary took his time answering. 'We didn't find out till later. It was a big Indian encampment – not a war camp, but a permanent village with families and cultivated fields. Place called Calico Creek. Later, Wyndham told us it was a disguised war camp and we had been ordered to destroy it.' He paused, took a deep breath. 'It was complete slaughter from the first mortar shell.'

'He . . . bombed women and children?' Dusty asked, horrified. Gary just stared back and suddenly she knew it hadn't just been torture in a prison camp that had made her uncle seek enduring and penitent solitude. 'What an awful thing to have to live with.'

Gary got up to pour coffee, hands shaking a little.

'You said my father saved all your lives,' prompted Fargo. Gary looked at him squarely. 'How?'

'We lost the rafts in some rapids after the slaughter. Two men drowned; another was crushed by logs. Tyson was trapped underwater, his leg caught between the logs, but Morg, the only one of us not badly injured, dived and saved him. He was a strong swimmer and he got us all ashore, one by one. Damn near killed himself doin' it. There was part of the raft still usable and he piled us aboard somehow, then stayed in the river, kicking and guiding the logs as best he could. It must've taken a hell of a lot out of him, but he got us to a sandy cove. Then, after resting, he walked off through some mighty rough country, came back with a bunch of Rebs and a couple of wagons.' Gary smiled thinly. 'We were all heroes, when we got back, of course, Wyndham the biggest, being the senior man. That was all hogwash about a "secret mission", too: we all knew it was Wyndham's own idea. He'd grabbed the chance to square things for what'd happened to his family. Trying out that new-type powder was the perfect excuse.'

They drank their coffee in silence, then Dusty asked, 'Was anyone ever called to account for the massacre?'

Gary said quietly, 'The Yankees got the blame. They denied it, of course, but several bloody Yankee uniforms, some side arms, and an officer's sabre were found amongst the bodies.' He paused, then nodded as it dawned on the others that Wyndham must've planted these, things that he'd ordered Tyson to gather earlier from the cavalry camp. 'Yeah, good ol' Cap'n Wyndham had it all worked out ahead of time. There was a good deal of outrage, and an investigation, but it didn't really matter – Wyndham got himself killed in one of the last battles of the war. The Calico Creek massacre never appeared in *any* kinda official report as such. The Yankees buried it deep and none of the squad ever said anything: we didn't want to be connected to it in any way.'

'Surely someone—' began an outraged Dusty, but Gary interrupted, shaking his head.

'It was one helluva mess just about that time. The war ended and all men wanted to do was go home, just dump their guns and walk away. I was one of 'em, wanted to forget all about the hell I'd been through and seen in those four years, specially that Indian camp.'

He sighed and another silence dragged until he said quietly, 'I came up here, away from everything, just to – hell, I dunno exactly *why* I came. Repenting in some way, I guess, by helpin' out the Indians where I could, and after all this time, that damn massacre's finally come back to kick me in the teeth!'

CHAPTER 12

NIGHT KILL

They decided to take turns at standing guard.

'I figure if Bisby's out there,' Lightfoot said, 'he's still got at least two men with him, mebbe three. One might be wounded, but we killed three others before they scattered ... I'm still not sure how many he started with.'

They drew straws to settle the sequence and Fargo pulled first duty, followed by Lightfoot, then Gary. Dusty wanted to take a turn but the men were adamant that she should stay put.

'Because I'm a woman!' she said testily.

'Yeah,' Gary said in clipped tones, clearly surprising her. Obviously she had expected some prevarication or beating about the bush. He suddenly smiled. 'You're a woman and my niece – my only living kin. That makes you kind of special.'

She sighed, actually pleased at his explanation, but

still a trifle miffed. 'If I'd been a *nephew* instead of a niece, I wonder if you'd take the same attitude?'

'Well, I reckon I ain't never gonna find out, so why don't you turn in? I got a little room in a lean-to I keep for occasional visitors . . . which I don't normally encourage. Lightfoot'll tell you the bunk's OK: he's used it.'

'It's fine, Dusty, no draughts,' the Indian said, looking mildly agitated. 'I'd feel better if we had a man out there right now on watch, Gary.'

He slid his dark eyes to Fargo, who nodded. Fargo checked his rifle, took the bottle of water Gary offered and glanced at Dusty. 'I figure I'll stay on with Gary a spell, Dusty. I've found him like my pa wanted and, well, all I've located before were dead men. I don't aim for it to happen again.'

Gary frowned slightly. 'I'm used to livin' alone – got my own ways. Likely kinda . . . queer to some folk.'

'Got *my* own ways, too,' Fargo said, smiling faintly. 'I don't think we'll get in each other's hair. Chief, can you see Dusty gets back home?'

Lightfoot nodded. 'I can, but it'd be better if she could stay at Barnabas for a few days.' Dusty looked a little startled and Fargo frowned, but Lightfoot went on. 'And Gary, don't you forget you gotta come down to the Reservation for the powwow. It's been put forward a week, as I told you.' He glanced at Fargo who was looking puzzled. 'I had to send my men back to start gettin' things ready for the arrival of the politicians, otherwise we'd have plenty of guards here.'

That made both Dusty and Fargo snap their heads up.

'What powwow's this?' the girl queried.

Gary looked uncomforable. 'Aw, this Senator Winfield is on some kinda political jaunt – tourin' around. S'posedly it'll count in his favour when it comes time to elect someone to stand up for us Indians, which, of course, will be Winfield. To make it look good, he's visitin' Indian Reservations and Agencies, showing his flag, sort of.'

'It's not only a welcome for him,' Lightfoot pointed out. *'You've* done a lot for my people, Gary. *A hell of a lot* – and we want to show our appreciation. Far as I'm concerned, the big powwow's more for you than this Winfield.'

Gary grimaced. 'I don't like bein' in the limelight.'

'Hell, we'd rather do it for you. I see Winfield as just another would-be politician cashin' in on behalf of his Eastern backers, who just happen to see potential profit in using us Indians as pawns *and* are powerful enough to ride him into the Senate. You just watch how they turn things to their own benefit once he's there.'

Gary still looked uneasy. Then Dusty said, 'I think the welcome is a great idea, Gary!' She turned to Lightfoot. 'But you sound quite sceptical of this Winfield. From what I've read and heard about him, he does have some very good ideas that'll benefit your people, Herb.'

'He says he has, but you got to remember he aims to be elected and tells folk what they want to hear. I reckon he's just a figurehead for a group in Washington who'll turn things to their own interests once he's voted in. It's bothered me for some time – I have someone looking into it, matter of fact. Should get some results pretty soon.'

Fargo frowned. 'He'll have a party line he'll have to follow, won't he? His "platform" I think they call it. What can he do?"

'Many things. But what worries me most – and the elders of the tribe – is our land. We've had to fight to keep what we have and there are powerful railroad men in the group sponsoring Winfield. I'll leave it at that. We'll be obliged to bend over backward to show our gratitude to the rich city men who supposedly have our interests at heart.'

There was a brief silence and Fargo said quietly, 'You're a born cynic, Chief.'

Lightfoot smiled wryly. 'I was born a Santee Sioux, Fargo.' And that was answer enough.

Fargo acknowledged the statement with a nod, gathered his things and went out into the night to take up his guard position.

Strangely, it was Dusty who heard the intruders first.

Gary had built the lean-to so that it was weather-proof against the torrential rain that often fell in that part of the country and the snows in winter. The result was that it was quite stuffy inside with the door closed. Dusty tossed and turned on the rawhide bunk. Finally, she decided she was too hot, even though the moun-tain air outside was on the chilly side.

Sleepily, she rolled out of the bunk, took the few steps to the door and lifted the latch. Gary was a good

132

carpenter, as she had noticed in his cabin and the trading post building itself, so the door made no noise when she eased it open. She stood there, feeling the slight chill of the mountain air on her heated body, deciding whether to leave the door fully open or just prop it ajar a few inches.

There were fewer night noises of animals up here in the high country, although she did hear the far-off howl of a wolf and a sound that might have been a bear downslope, forcing his way through brush. This last thought gave her a twitch in the stomach and she decided that maybe she could stand the stuffiness of the small compartment after all. . . .

Then there was a different sound – an unmistakable sound she had heard hundreds of times on Slash S: the tinkling jingle of spur rowels.

And she knew Fargo, on guard, did not wear spurs. . . .

It came from down the slope, about ten yards away. She hesitated briefly, then turned swiftly back into the lean-to, fumbling in the dark to find where she had left her Colt revolver close to the head of the bunk. She knocked over the crate that was acting as a bedside table and there was a loud clatter as the gun fell off.

Heart hammering, she set the crate upright and groped around the immediate area for the weapon. Her hand touched the butt just as she heard a footstep behind her. She whirled as a strange voice said,

'Well, smoke me, Blink! I b'lieve I do smell a woman in here!'

'Keep your voice down!' rasped someone else in the

133

darkness, sounding a mite breathless – from the climb up the slope, probably.

By then Dusty had decided the best thing she could do was scream her head off. And she did exactly that.

'*Jesus*! Grab her!'

The man who rushed at her was no more than a darker movement against the blackness. She tripped over the crate and sprawled across the narrow bunk, rapping her head against one of the uprights. She saw stars and dragged down air for another scream. Then a pair of iron-hard arms encircled her upper body and lifted her, swinging her around. Dusty's lower legs clipped the bunk upright again, causing her more brief pain.

'Got her, Blink! An' she's a hellcat! Just the way I like 'em!'

'Shut her up, dammit! By hell, Mo, you know what Al's like on a job! He finds out you messed this up just because of some piece of ass. . . .'

Mo was gasping for breath as Dusty fought and struggled, her legs kicking the air, throwing him off balance. 'Goddammit, woman! Quit that!'

He flung her down across the bunk and back-handed her brutally. She went limp. Mo struggled with his belt buckle.

'Mo! Christ, man, are you loco! It's a wonder Sloane ain't out here right now. . . .'

'He's not – but I am!' a voice said behind him.

Blink grunted as a rifle barrel slammed across the back of his head, knocking him to his knees against the door frame. Mo spun away from the bunk, whipping his hand from his belt buckle to his gunbutt. He dropped to one knee and triggered, the flash briefly lighting the lean-to as thunder bounced off the cramping walls. Dusty glimpsed Blink sprawled across the doorway, Fargo jumping sideways as Mo's shot whined off the door frame.

Then Fargo stepped back, half-crouched, and his rifle crashed in two fast shots. Dusty heard Mo grunt as his body was slammed up against the sloping roof. He fell to his knees and toppled sideways. She found herself crouching on the bunk having no recollection of climbing there, blinking, trying to get her eyes used to the darkness after the searing gunflashes. She couldn't see clearly but the powderflash had reflected from a six-gun as the half-conscious Blink struggled in the doorway.

'Watch out!' she cried and Fargo instantly dropped to one knee, swinging the rifle around, lever blurring as it jacked a shell into the breech. The sound of the shot over-rode that of the six-gun as Fargo lurched, grabbing at the door frame to keep from falling.

Blink was stretched out on the floor, no longer interested in trying to shoot anyone, blood on his chest.

Dusty clambered off the bunk, sidled past Mo's unmoving body, and jumped as a match flared.

'You OK?'

She breathed a sigh of relief as Fargo asked his question. 'Yes, I'm all right. How about you?'

'I've got a splinter from the door just under the ribs. No real damage.'

By that time Lightfoot and Gary had arrived, the latter carrying a shotgun, which he believed was the best weapon to use at night. Lightfoot held his rifle and stared at the two bodies in the light of the lantern Dusty had lit.

'This one's still alive,' Gary said, kneeling beside Blink. 'Not for long, though, I suspect.'

'Long enough to tell us a few things, I hope,' said Fargo. 'But after we take a look around – Al Bisby's probably still out there somewhere.'

'Me and Lightfoot'll take a look,' Gary said.

As they started out, Fargo trained his rifle on the wounded man. But he didn't think he was playing possum, not with all that blood on his chest.

Dusty knelt beside him, trying to staunch the flow of blood. Fargo held the lantern close to the grey, pain-lined face.

'Blink Thomas! I saw him when I passed through Deadwood a while back. He was a deputy sheriff then – blinks every time a gun goes off, they say.'

Thomas's eyes fluttered open and he looked up at Dusty and Fargo, his gaze seeming slightly out of focus.

'They – they said you were – just a – kid.'

'I am,' Fargo agreed, adding, 'a tough kid. Why'd you turn in your badge, Blink? You were doin' all right in Deadwood from what I heard.'

'M-money – why you think? Like to gamble.'

Blink was breathing hard, the air mixing with blood and mucus and rattling in his upper chest with each word.

'Well, you put your life on the line this time.'

'He needs a doctor,' Dusty said quietly, but Blink Thomas surprised her by moving his head negatively, side to side, his blood-flecked lips parting in what could have been a faint smile.

'Never make it, Miss. Sorry I couldn't keep Mo away from you.'

She gently wiped sweat from his brow. 'You'd be better off not talking.'

'We need him to talk, Dusty,' Fargo said.

She gave him a hard look and whispered fiercely, 'The man's severely wounded! Surely he's entitled to a little peace!'

'Mebbe, but he hasn't always been as docile as this. He's got a rep for shooting people almost as big as Bisby, only he had a badge to back him up.'

'Al beats me in the body count,' grunted Blink, fighting hard to say something else. 'I – I can't tell you anythin' you'd wanna hear, Fargo. I din' ask questions – just – just sold out for a heap of *dinero* an' that's all.' He grimaced as pain shot through him, breathing as if he had just run a mile. It changed to a wracking cough and both Fargo and Dusty moved quickly to avoid the spray of blood.

'Who paid you, Blink?' Fargo asked. 'Who wanted all those men dead? Gary's the only one left now and Bisby's still after him. I want to know why.'

Thomas stared straight up into Fargo's face. His eyes were dulling. His mouth worked, and whatever he said came out in a harsh, ragged whisper. He tried to lift his head a little, then flopped back, the whites of his eyes showing, the sucking wound in his chest silent now as his breathing abruptly stopped. Dark blood trickled over his sagging chin.

Dusty, white-faced now as she moved back, still looking down at the dead man, asked, 'What did he say?'

Fargo answered slowly. 'I'm not certain sure but I *think* he said "Wyndham's footing the bill". . . .'

CHAPTER 13

GATHERING STORM

'You must've heard wrong,' Gary Sloane told Fargo emphatically. 'Told you, Wyndham was killed just before the end of the war.'

Fargo lifted the glass of whiskey Gary had poured and tossed it down. 'More I think of it, Gary, more certain I am that's what Blink said: "Wyndham's footin' the bill".'

'Is there some other name that might've sounded like "Wyndham"?' asked Lightfoot.

Fargo looked at Sloane, who frowned, hesitated, then said, 'Was gonna say Winfield but it doesn't sound quite like Wyndham. Anyway, not likely to be him, bein' a politician and in the public's eye all the time.'

'How about you, Dusty?' Fargo asked the quiet,

sober girl. 'Now you've had time to think about it. . . ?'

She stared, tight-lipped, then shook her head slightly.

'I didn't hear it clearly at all. He was dying and his breathing was noisy, rattling. A horrible sound.' She stopped, absently rubbing at a bloodstain on her blouse. 'But I still think Wyndham's the closest.'

'Don't make sense!' Gary snapped, on the edge of being outright annoyed. 'He died in a fight with Yankees who were using Sioux Indians alongside the soldiers. Always figured it was kinda appropriate, the Sioux finishing off an Injun-hater like him.' He tapped his fingers on the edge of the table, aware the others were watching him closely. He sighed. 'OK, I s'pose it's possible it wasn't Wyndham they found, but if he did somehow survive, where the hell is the son of a bitch now?'

Gary, plainly unsettled, took his shotgun and made for the door. He stopped with it halfway open. 'I'll check around again. I'd like to get my hands on this Bisby and find out just what the hell's goin' on.' Agitated, unthinking, he stood silhouetted against the lamplight – a good target.

Fargo tensed. 'Gary! Get outta the doorway!'

As he spoke, there was a single rifle shot from outside and Sloane grunted, head jerking violently as he spun around, cap spinning off and bears' teeth scattering from the headband as he collapsed. Dusty screamed and Fargo kicked over his chair, sweeping up his rifle and diving through the doorway, scrambling to one side. A second shot thudded into the door. Dusty and Lightfoot dragged Gary back into the cabin as Fargo called from the darkness, 'Time you gave up, Bisby, you murderin' swine!'

A voice answered from up the slope. 'I got a bead on you, too, Fargo!'

By now Fargo was crouched behind a rainwater barrel, but held his fire. 'You can't see me, Bisby!'

'Try movin', you'll find out!'

Fargo was already moving, belly-down, in sinewy, snake-like movements with co-ordinated elbows and knees. Stealth was something he had learned from the Australian Aborigines: you were absolutely silent sneaking up on an animal or you went hungry – and on the bleak island where they lived that was not an option.

'Hey! You wouldn't be tryin' to sneak up on me, would you?' Bisby suddenly sounded worried. He fired a wild shot. Fargo heard the bullet thud into the rain barrel. Water spurted, the sound covering his own progress as he moved more swiftly now. 'I can hear better'n an Injun even while talkin' my head off an'— *Holy Mike!* Where'd you. . . !'

Bisby jumped up from his crouched position, shooting from the hip. But Fargo was slightly above him now. Gravel stung his face but he didn't flinch as he dropped the killer with two quick shots. He held the smoking rifle on the thrashing figure until Bisby was still though coughing wetly.

Ju-das! I messed up that one, din' I! Never was much with a rifle! Six-gun square-off was my style.'

'Not any more, Al,' Fargo said now standing over

141

him. 'You're bleedin' bad. Don't think you'll make it.'

'Bastard! Listen – I got – I got a wife an' a boy in Wacco. Go by name of Allen. Will – will you see they get the money Winfield owes me? They – they think I'm – a trail driver.'

'You've got a damn hide askin' me this! You were goin' to blow my head off a minute ago.'

Bisby was gasping for breath, as he reached up with one bloody hand and clawed at Fargo's shirt. 'No one else to ask. I ain't got long, but I can tell you a few things.'

It was obvious that Bisby wouldn't live much longer, so Fargo said, 'That list of names . . . I've figured it has to be something to do with that massacre Wyndham pulled at Calico Creek.' Bisby stared up with pain-racked eyes, snorting breaths now. 'If word got out Winfield was involved he'd never get elected.'

Bisby coughed up blood. When he settled he said, 'He did it, for Chris'sakes!'

'Win*field*? Or Wynd*ham*?'

'Same man.'

Fargo stopped with his mouth partly open. 'Wyndham survived that battle at the end of the war?'

'Was never in it. Just a uniform an' his papers on some poor luckless sonuver. . . .' His words slurred away.

Bisby's eyes were slowly glazing, his speech thickening, attention wandering. Fargo gripped him by one shoulder. 'So Wyndham the Indian-hater became Winfield, the Indian-lover?'

That almost made Bisby laugh but it turned into another body-shaking cough. His voice was very harsh and wheezy when he spoke. 'Once he's in, to hell with the Injuns. He'll get their land made available for the railroads.'

'Already figured that. And where there's railroads, land prices are sky high, so everyone makes a big profit.'

The bloody hand once again tugged at Fargo's arm – urgently. Bisby tried to sit up, a desperate look on his pain-twisted face. 'My boy, he's smart – deserves a chance. I – never had one, I only knew – how to – shoot – fast.' His voice became more urgent. 'See – he gets what's owed me. He don't have to know it's blood money.' He fell back, chest heaving, almost choking as internal bleeding filled his lungs. 'Wife neither. . . .'

Fargo grabbed the red hand. 'I'll see they're OK.'

He thought the man smiled through all that blood before drawing his last, shuddering breath. . . .

He jerked his gun up, startled, as Lightfoot spoke close behind him. 'I come to see if you're all right and find you doing a favour for the man who just tried to kill you!'

'You're well-named, by God! Never heard you at all. Yeah, Bisby was a murdering son of a bitch but there's no point lettin' his family suffer because of it.'

'Well, you are something . . . different, Fargo.'

'Never mind me – how's Gary?'

'We're moving him to Barnabas. Breck's almost as good as a doctor. Scalp wound's not too bad.'

Gary still hadn't come round fully when they rode into Barnabas that afternoon. The place was crawling with

Indians, hundreds of them: the usual Reservation population had doubled. They wore all kinds of feathered headdresses and decorated buckskin clothes, ready to take part in the big powwow, a carnival to be performed especially for Winfield and his political backers – The *Progress Party*.

'Winfield and his outfit are on their way,' Breck told him. 'We have a small infirmary where we can treat Gary – successfully, I hope. Oh, Herb, there's a package for you, too, came on the stage. The envelope has us intrigued: there's a sketch of a large eye with the words: "*We never sleep*".'

Lightfoot smiled. 'Sign and motto of the Pinkerton Detective Agency. I've had them investigating Winfield and his party for quite a while.'

'Allan Pinkerton?' Dusty asked. 'I've heard of him – he saved Lincoln from an assassination attempt some time ago and is supposed to've set up the first Yankee espionage unit behind Rebel lines in the war. He's quite famous.'

'That's him. A Scot with an accent you couldn't cut with a knife, but he has high integrity and claims he always gets his man. I'll read his report while Breck works on Gary.'

Despite their concerns about the visiting Progress Party, and its suspect candidate for election, Dusty and Fargo took time to watch the Indians in a full dress rehearsal for the big powwow. Fargo thought it would help take her mind off her worries about her uncle.

The colours were eye-dazzling: a whirling kaleidoscope of feathered headdresses moved in traditional formations to the throb of beating hide drums; shrill tunes of bird-bone whistles; the tinkling of wrist and ankle bells. The dances looked complicated but it was soon apparent that every participant knew his routine and performed it faultlessly. Children, too, took part. Well-fed painted faces set serious in concentration came alive with laughter and brilliant smiles, once they had mastered their routines.

The warriors were more serious and intent. Fargo sensed that many of them would rather this gathering wasn't seen as a mere circus for the pleasure of uninitiated whites but rather what it was originally intended to be: a demonstration of their dedication to the old traditional Indian ways that no white man could ever really savvy – or change.

After the performance, they found Lightfoot sitting in his teepee on a colourful blanket, surrounded by scattered pages.

'Pinkerton's as thorough as he claims. It'll save time if I tell you what he's written. You can read it later.' He shuffled pages. He says Winfield's real name is definitely Wyndham, but he believes they could be brothers.'

'They can't be brothers.' Both men looked sharply at Dusty. 'Gary said Wyndham's deranged hatred of Indians was because they'd tortured and wiped out *his entire family* – parents and all his siblings. He was the only one left.'

'Dusty's right, Chief. According to Al Bisby, Winfield and Wyndham are one and the same man.'

Lightfoot's eyes narrowed. 'So! A genuine Indian-hater, hiding under the guise of an outspoken Indian-*lover*! I guess you'd call it a pretty smart move.'

'And one of the reasons he hired Bisby to kill off the survivors of the massacre at Calico Creek. If it ever got out he instigated it, well, that sort of thing can bring down a whole government, let alone one political party.'

Dusty looked horrified. 'My God! What kind of men are they?'

'Ruthless, Dusty,' Lightfoot told her grimly. He waved the paper he held. 'It's all in here – Pinkerton points out several places where he's conjecturing for lack of solid proof, but the facts he uses make it almost certain he's right in every case. It's all a sham to get Winfield into the Senate where he can do what they tell him.'

'They must've trained him for years,' Dusty said.

The Indian nodded slowly. 'Yes, getting him the right contacts and background. He's had a long career on the edge of politics, been well groomed in party policies and dirty tricks. Once he's in, he'll be a very powerful man.'

'And a rich one,' allowed Fargo.

'Yes, while we Indians are crammed on to Reservations that probably won't support grass, let alone enough fertile land for crops and graze for cattle!'

Lightfoot made no attempt to hide his bitterness as he looked at the very probable future of his people. His hands were shaking as he held the pages, his anger mounting.

'Well, Chief, if you're satisfied with Pinkerton's report, we have to decide what the hell to do – and not take too damn long about it.'

The decision was easy enough: denounce Winfield-Wyndham and do it while so many tribes were gathered here. Let them see their votes were being bought with false promises and lies by a man half-out of his head with hatred – for them. It could get out of hand – but better now than later, when Winfield had the whole political party backing him. They were behind him now, but would have much more clout once he was officially elected to the Senate. *Now* was a good time to prevent that.

But ... *someone* had quietly distributed whiskey among the tribes – the genuine article, not the rotgut usually peddled and foisted upon the unsuspecting red men.

'I'm afraid that whiskey is one aspect of the white man's way of life that's welcomed by my people,' Lightfoot said with a hard edge of sadness. 'I should've realized something like this would happen. It's calculated to help sway the vote in Winfield's favour.'

'Don't blame yourself, Chief. There's such a helluva crowd here they can get away with it and easily deny any knowledge if it's discovered.'

Dusty looked apprehensive as she watched capering, staggering braves laughing and behaving stupidly, some quite belligerently, already more than half-drunk or half-wild. 'Will they become violent?'

'Among themselves, maybe,' Lightfoot murmured.

'I don't think they'll start anything too rough as long as the Progress Party keeps them supplied with whiskey.' He paused. 'Now *there's* a name for you! "progress!" Just where the hell are we supposed to be "progressing" to!'

'Take it easy, Chief,' Fargo said, a little alarmed to see Lightfoot getting so worked up, even though he savvied the man's reaction and couldn't blame him.

'Easy? I can't stand by and allow my people to be manipulated in this way! How I see it, it's worth *any* risk, even of an uprising, to head this off right now.'

Fargo grabbed the big Indian's arm as he made to swing away. The dark eyes blazed at him. 'Let go, Fargo!'

'Come see Gary first.'

Lightfoot frowned. 'Gary? Well, I hope Breck has done him some good, but his welfare will have to take second place until I—'

'Wait, Chief, dammit! Gary knows more about this than any of us. He was there at Calico Creek. Let him and Winfield meet face to face. See if Gary recognizes him. Just now the only thing we know is that Al Bisby *said* Winfield and Wyndham are the same man. If he was just talking off the top of his head, we could have an entirely wrong slant on things.'

'Look at those fools!' Lightfoot gritted, staring out the open doorflap. 'Proud warriors? By the gods! It's no better than the drunks in the back streets of Denver and other big towns! I don't want my people reduced to suchf . . . shame! I *must* put a stop to it and I intend to—'

'Chief Lightfoot,' cautioned Dusty suddenly. 'You should remember Mr Breck said Winfield always travels with three heavily armed bodyguards.'

The Indian glanced at Fargo who nodded agreement.

'Then we'll check our guns first,' Lightfoot said, tight lipped.

CHAPTER 14

LEGACY

Senator-elect Winfield and his team arrived in mid-afternoon. No fanfare of blaring bugles or a volley of gunshots, but then they weren't needed, because Winfield's specially built coach was painted red, white and blue, with scattered silver stars and slogan banners stretched on each side: *PROGRESS FOR ALL AMERICANS!*

There was a tobacco-chewing, squint-eyed shotgun guard riding up beside the driver, scanning for dangers. There were also three out-riders, one out front on a black horse; two more, one each side. All were dressed in good-quality range clothes, the one in front sporting twin-holstered six-guns, the others with single Colts. All looked dangerous and serious about their job: the bodyguarding of Martin Winfield.

Behind this colourful coach there was a second, not so garish, but in fresh maroon, yellow-trimmed paint and again, a prominent shotgun guard, thrusting an iron jaw forward as he looked around constantly. Inside were four well-fed city-dressed men wearing Derby hats, with glittering stick-pins in their yellow and green cravats – the colours of the Progress Party.

There may have been a touch of apprehension in their faces when they saw the solid mass of Indians crowding close as the vehicles skidded to a halt. A dapper little man burst from the door of the red, white and blue coach before it came properly to a halt, folded down the step and stood stiffly beside it. When the vehicle had stopped rocking a man in striped trousers and grey frockcoat over a fancy vest and white silk shirt stepped down, looking around with a fixed smile in place. He was of medium height and lifted his white hat with its precisely curled brim, revealing grey-streaked hair plastered flat with glistening pomade. His smile broadened as he looked carefully around at the bunched, staring Indians, then he threw his arms wide.

'Well, *howdy, fellow Americans!*' he shouted loudly, fashionable mutton-chop whiskers fairly bristling. 'I'm Martin Winfield and with your votes behind me, I'm heading to Washington to change your lives! *For the better!*'

He waited for the anticipated cheer, but, while Progress men were scattered at strategic places among the crowd, at best it was no more than a few grunts and an occasional '*Hah-ya!*'

But it takes more than that to get under the iron hide of a practising politician on the make, and

Winfield slid easily into his act. He stepped down to the ground and began to mix with the Indians, grabbing their hands and pumping vigorously, saying brief words of encouragement, few of which were understood, let alone heeded. But he moved on through the crowd, watched a mite anxiously by the four Progress committee members from inside their own coach. . . .

Cameron Breck, hastily dressed in decent clothes after his surgical work on Gary Sloane, hurried up and introduced himself, adding, 'Welcome to Barnabas, Mr Winfield.'

'Thank you, Agent Breck – soon to be *Senator* Winfield, I hope!'

'I wish you luck, sir. It's far too noisy here – would you care to come into our assembly hall, wash the dust out of your throat?'

'I'm your man!' Winfield winked broadly: those words were his election slogan: *I'm Your Man!*

It was a spacious hall with a low roof, which tended to make the atmosphere a little stuffy. Breck had men on the door who kept the crowd to a minimum so there was room to move about and let the air circulate. There was a mild altercation while the three outriders pushed their way past Breck's men. Winfield noticed and said quietly to Breck,

'My bodyguards – I'm committed to having them within sight at all times, Agent Breck.'

Breck hurried to sort things out and when he returned said, diplomatically, 'While we're waiting for the table to be readied, er, Senator,' this produced a sober nod from Winfield, 'I'd like you to meet some friends.'

'Certainly! Friends are always desirable, and *good* friends, well, who can put a value on someone who has earned one's trust and affection, eh?'

Typical, sweet-talking, mealy-mouthed jayhawker! Lightfoot thought as Dusty was introduced first. Winfield, of course, gave her a courtly bow and lifted one of her work-caloused hands, lightly brushing his lips across the knuckles. 'Your servant, ma'am.'

Before the flustered girl could think of anything to say, Breck said, 'And this is Craig Fargo.'

Lightfoot watched closely as Fargo was announced and saw a sudden wariness in Winfield's eyes, which the man swiftly covered as he enthusiastically shook hands.

'I believe I have heard that name – are you related to the famous stageline, sir?'

'No such luck, Mr Winfield.' Fargo may or may not have meant to emphasize the 'mister' but the way he said it, tightened up Winfield's smile.

The three bodyguards stared expressionlessly, looking relaxed with thumbs hooked into belt buckles – only inches away from their Colts. Fargo returned the stares frankly. Left to right they were: Paulie McCann, thin-faced, lean as a whip, eyes like bullets; Burt Reno, his thin moustache enhancing the Mexican ancestry in his swarthy, quite handsome features; and, finally, the big man with flaring nostrils, the coarse-skinned nose, and a beard trimmed to a point: Dakota Evans, said to be unable to ever return to his home state because of his misdeeds. All three names had come up a few times during Fargo's search.

They gave him the once-over, unsmiling, unimpressed.

Then Lightfoot, who had excused himself for a moment, returned, pushing Gary Sloane in a wheelchair. Gary's head was bandaged and his hands rested limply on a light blanket covering his legs. His face, drawn and grey, brought a gasp of concern from Dusty, but Fargo stopped her as she made to step towards her uncle.

Breck introduced Lightfoot to Winfield who shook his hand enthusiastically enough, though only for a brief moment. The politician's eyes went to Gary who regarded him silently.

Breck said, slightly hesitant, 'May I introduce Gary Sloane, Senator? One of our agency's mentors. Er, he has recently been wounded but insisted on meeting you.'

Winfield was sober and wary now, but recovered quickly, putting out his overworked right hand, 'Gary, very pleased to meet anyone who has sympathy and compassion for our cause and who acknowledges the long-time plight of our red brothers. I trust your wound is none too serious. . . ?'

Gary took the proferred hand and when Winfield made to withdraw it speedily, tightened his grip. Winfield frowned, glancing towards his bodyguards, Fargo noticed. He nudged Lightfoot who nodded very slightly without looking at him.

Gary, in a weak, strained voice, looked straight into

Winfield's tightening face: 'We've met before.'

'I – don't believe so, sir. I have a quite fantastic memory for faces but I cannot recall yours.'

'Well, I was a deal younger then, and I used to salute you instead of shakin' hands, Captain.'

Winfield's smile was freezing by the second now. He glanced at his alert bodyguards, then tried to rally with, 'Colonel, actually. I attained that rank before I left the army, but I don't use the title in civilian life.'

No: the army connection would not go down well when a man was trying to ride into the White House as being pro-Indian. . . .

'When I knew you, you were captain of a mortar squad – in the 15th Light Artillery, Sawatch Brigade.'

Winfield had managed to regain his control now and smiled indulgently, shaking his head. 'You are mistaken, my friend. I was a cavalry officer for my entire army career – I suppose it's possible we may've met briefly. My Company supported various groups, though I do not immediately recall any mortar squad that we—'

'You ought to!' Gary broke in hoarsely and Fargo tensed, seeing Lightfoot do the same. 'I was one of your spotters – the other being Fargo's father. He was your sergeant and we raided a Yankee cavalry encampment at Hellfire Bend. I knew you as Captain Mark Wyndham, then. . . .'

The three bodyguards looked as if they were standing on coiled springs, waiting to be hurled into the inevitable violence that was clearly coming. Breck started to speak but no one even looked at him and he chewed his bottom lip worriedly as Winfield, frowning, said, 'I don't understand any of this, Chief Lightfoot. Why your man is so hostile, I can't even begin to guess. Obviously he shouldn't be out of his sick bed. But can we move along, perhaps? I have a very tight schedule and—'

'It's gonna get tighter!' Gary said breathlessly, squirming a little in the wheelchair. 'Like a hangman's noose!'

'Dammit, Chief! I've put up with enough of this! I don't know this man or what he's trying to say. I want—'

'C'mon, Wyndham!' croaked Gary again, body shuddering with his breaths, pushing Dusty aside with one hand as she leaned towards him, never taking his hot gaze off Winfield. 'You remember me, all right, and all the others you took to Calico Creek before ordering us to bomb an Indian settlement out of existence! Women and kids along with the warriors, because years earlier, some other Indians had wiped out your family!'

There was dead silence in the big hall: the red men who were present stared hard at Winfield, knowing well the dreadful massacre of Calico Creek. The whites were on their toes, the women – and some men – looking mighty worried at this turn of events. . . .

Winfield was momentarily speechless. The guards were stretched nerve-taut, waiting only for their employer's signal to go for their guns. Fargo and Lightfoot were as tense as Winfield and Breck knelt beside Gary, trying to calm the wounded man down as he sat wild-eyed and clenching the wheel rims of his wheelchair.

'You made us wait behind while you went to see for yourself, all those women and their kids blown to bloody shreds by our mortars! You gonna tell the people you want to vote for you about that?'

'Lightfoot!' Winfield almost screamed, his control at breaking point now, sweat streaming down his face. *Then his left foot lifted* and the instep rapidly massaged the muscle of his other leg. Gary's eyes almost popped. 'I – I did not come here to be insulted, accused of some atrocity that happened almost twenty years ago. I've never even heard of this damn Calico Creek!'

Suddenly the room was as still and as quiet as the inside of a coffin. *The entire country had been aghast after news of the Calico Creek massacre leaked out. The Yankees did their best to bury it – but too late: everyone knew enough to be horrified, even though the end of the war soon pushed it into the background. So denying having even heard of Calico Creek put all of Winfield's protests into doubt. . . .*

He made several attempts to speak, but it was obvious few would believe his stammering bluster now.

'No good, Wyndham!' snapped Gary, breathlessly. 'Apart from anything else, that left foot rubbing your other leg was a dead giveaway! Ask anyone who'd ever heard of Captain Mark Wyndham. It was a joke with the soldiers, a trade mark: "Wyndham's Wiggle" they called it.'

Sweat was pouring down Winfield's face now. His lips were trembling and he reached into his coat. '*You bastard!*' he gritted, as he brought out an over-under derringer and, fired both barrels, one after the other, into Gary Sloane. Sloane was rammed back in his chair, but flame stabbed through the light blanket over his legs, causing the cloth to smoulder as the crowds scattered and the room erupted into panic. Gary, struggling, brought out a slim Navy Colt and fired a shot into Winfield's stomach. The would-be senator screamed and clutched at his blood-spurting wound as his knees folded and he thudded to the floor. Gary slumped back, sliding down a little in the chair. . . .

By that time the bodyguards had spread out and their guns hammered. Lightfoot reeled as a bullet struck him and he fired his own gun in a wild shot that took Paulie McCann in the throat. The man clutched at it, staggering drunkenly. Both Reno and Evans froze in shock as blood spurted copiously from their colleague.

That moment of shock was all that Fargo needed. He dived forward, grabbing Dusty and thrusting her beneath a table before rolling out the other side and coming up on to one knee. He fanned his hammer, not four feet away from Evans. The big man staggered as three bullets slammed into his body.

He twisted as he fell, gun blasting, and Burt Reno stepped quickly behind him, grabbing him under one arm and using his body as a shield as he triggered at Fargo. But Fargo was no longer where he had been a split second before.

He shoulder-rolled and as he came up, fired his last shot, even as Reno spun towards him. The half-breed

Mexican's head snapped back on his neck as if it would fly off, his good looks destroyed, now only blood and gristle. . . .

The chaos in the smoke-filled room took a good deal of settling down – the guests, both red and white, shouting and jostling, desperately trying to squeeze out through the narrow doorways. When some order was finally regained, Winfield was dead, as were his bodyguards – and Gary Sloane. Breck had a bullet graze across one cheek; Lightfoot had a chest wound but the lead had struck at an angle and torn out through his flesh without doing much real damage. He would be sore for a long time but would recover.

Fargo helped Dusty out from under the table. She stared at him with wide eyes. Her mouth worked but no words came.

'It's all right, Dusty,' he told her. 'This'll take some sorting out but it'll be all right.'

She nodded, taking a deep breath. 'We'd better see to our . . . wounded,' she said, shaking despite her efforts, her eyes filling with tears as she looked at the huddled body of her uncle.

Fargo slipped an arm about her waist, holding her firmly. 'Yeah, lucky there weren't more casualties. You think I could take over Gary's trading post deal? I like these mountains and I'd carry on his work. It's be a worthwhile legacy I reckon – if you agree?'

'I'm sure Uncle Gary would approve. When will you move in?' She dabbed at her eyes, fighting the urge to break into full-blown grief.

'After I get back from Waco, I guess.'

She blinked. 'Waco, Texas? Why do you have to go there?'

'Long story,' he said, catching Lightfoot's eye. The man winked slowly even as he grimaced at a stab of pain.

'He – promised a man to – deliver something,' the Indian said, looking at Fargo. 'Incidentally, how will you get the money?'

'Those four "Progress" committeemen or whatever you call them – I reckon they'd rather pay a few thousand than have all the details of the Calico Creek massacre given to every newspaper in Colorado – and beyond. Their involvement in trying to suppress them wouldn't do them any good.'

Lightfoot smiled and nodded as he turned to Dusty. 'See, Dusty? Fargo's a man of his word: he says he'll do something, he does it.'

Dusty nodded, almost smiling. She wouldn't really understand until she learned about Fargo having given his word to Al Bisby. Even then she might not approve, but the part she was remembering now, was that Fargo had said a few moments earlier:

'*After I get back. . . .*'

Library Link Issues (For Staff Use Only)

1	2	3	4	5	6	7	8	9
							$51A$	

8093 lm 01/04